Gemstone Series
Book One

The Emerald Lady

This is a work of fiction. Names, characters, places and incidents either are the product of the author's imagination or are used fictitiously, and any resemblance to any actual persons, living or dead, events, or locales is entirely coincidental.

Revised 6/23/2017

Published By

RockHill Publishing LLC
PO Box 62241
Virginia Beach, VA 23466-2241
www.rockhillpublishing.com

The Emerald Lady

James L Hill

TABLE OF CONTENT

Dedication

She pulls her veil across the Earth

Silently exposing the Universe in all her beauty

Thanks to you

My Ancient Muse

Thundering heartbeats

Pumps fire through my veins

My soul's alive

With Muse's Love

The years turn gray and eyes do dim

A hand reaches from then

To now

Forever My Muse

Chapter 1
Shipwreck

Jack Roggies was a twelve-year-old ship's boy. Young for the position, being two to four years prior to the normal, but he was hard working even if lacking the strength needed to haul water to the men on deck. Nevertheless, he was spry and agile as someone his age should be, able to avoid getting in the way of the men working the lines and sheets. Also, quick to respond to anyone's call, and not just Captain Meyers or Midshipman Simmons, he had earned his nickname, Jack Quick, by being the fastest to reach the Fore Royal Mast, and was best suited for the job of ship's lookout.

Jack was in awe of the enormous size of the Rummy Gale, the biggest ship in Portsmouth, and had to learn all the stores quickly, going up and down the four lower decks, running the 220-feet bow to aft and being reminded constantly, in his first week at sea, that all things must be done on the double.

The Rummy Gale was a Dutch-built Indiaman, large and heavy, made for hauling cargo. She had seen better days at sea but she was still steady in her timbers, and had recently gone through a careening for a thorough cleaning and tarring. She was a solid 1,422-ton beast of the sea empty but on this voyage, she was hauling two hundred tons of lumber. As a result, she was riding a little low, as noted by the Captain.

Jack called down from his perch 187-feet above the deck, "dark clouds on the horizon dead ahead. I see God's anger."

"Give a heading to steer clear," called the Midshipman.

"No clearing, Mr. Simmons, solid wall from end to end. Lots of heaven's fire too."

"Come down, boy. A storm can be upon us quicker than even you can climb," yelled the Captain.

"Aye, aye, Captain." Jack started down the shroud. Descending to the foremast, he spotted something off starboard, and hooking his arm through the ropes, he pulled the spyglass from his trousers, scanned the waves alongside the ship, and noticed a bloody red body appear and sink below the waves. He yelled, "man overboard, off starboard!"

Jeremy Simmons raced to the gunwale, several sailors taking up position along the side also, all searching for a man in the water.

The Captain called up. "Give a bearing, boy!"

Jack pointed towards the bow, "it was there, Sir! A league distance, streaked with blood and tossed in the waves."

The Captain scanned from where the boy pointed backwards. "Do any of you men see it, or any debris in the water?"

A chorus of, "nay," rumbled down the length of the ship.

The Captain looked across the horizon through his spyglass and ordered the boy back up the shroud to his perch with instructions to be on watch for a ship's mast. Then he called Jeremy Simmons over. "Don't keep him aloft too long, and keep a lookout for any sign of a shipwreck on the horizon."

"What's your thinking, Captain?"

"I'm thinking that a boy his age should not be on my ship, Mr. Simmons. It is a fine age for the navy, who can afford to train a boy to be an officer and a gentleman. But this is a commercial ship, I cannot afford to pay a boy who can't earn his keep."

"Yes, Sir. But as I explained before we embarked, his father died and he is the eldest of his mother's sons. He needs to earn a crossing wage, if the family is to survive, so he will be my responsibility." Then wanting to veer the conversation in another direction, Jeremy asked. "What about the body in the water?"

3

"I saw no body," stated Captain Meyers, "what's more, I see no wreckage that would accompany a body this far out. Did you?"

"No, Sir." Jeremy agreed.

"My thinking is; this is the first of many storms we will encounter on this passage, and a boy just from his mother's teat is full of fear of what a storm at sea brings. As right he should be. If he does not spot a mast hiding among the clouds, or any wreckage in the waves soon, send him below to ride out the storm."

The Captain knew that a body in the water, unaccompanied by any other sign of wreckage, was a known pirate's trick to get a ship to luff and becalm her sails. Then they would come racing out of the coverage of the storm and take the ship while it was busy rescuing a person long-time dead. Likewise, the absence of another ship could be a sign of something even more dangerous to come.

As the bank of black clouds appeared before the Rummy Gale, Jeremy Simmons ordered Jack Quick from the riggings, and replaced him with other sailors reefing the upper sails in preparation for the storm. Thunder rolled across the waves and Jack shuddered as he, and Jeremy made their way to the Captain's quarters.

Jeremy, towering over the frail boy, placed a firm hand on his shoulder, "a storm is a storm, the same at sea as on land. It is just a bit of wind, water, and wailing. Calm yourself, Jack."

"Yes Sir."

"Oh, but it is not just a storm when you are at sea." The Captain contradicted the midshipman, as he stood in the cabin's doorway watching the men prepare. The waves already rocking the ship even as heavy as she was.

The storm was still several hours ahead, but Jack was right, it stretched from port to starboard with not a break in sight and he hoped the wall of black did not go on for too long. Jeremy had convinced him that carrying milled lumber would increase the load and therefore the profit of the voyage, but it also meant that the ship was much heavier, ride lower in the waves, and be more prone to sinking in a violent storm. "On land, a storm does not open the ground beneath your feet and pull you under. Now, what did you see from your lookout, Master Roggies?"

"You mean the body," Jack said carefully, as he was quite afraid of the Captain. The grey beard was rugged and unkempt, and the face hard and scarred. "I saw a body with long streaks of blood down its back. But the blood was bright crimson, like fire, it was there for but a moment, then gone."

The Captain led them into his cabin and poured the young boy a full glass of grog. Four times his daily ration. Then he lit up his pipe, taking several strong pulls to get it going. Smoke whorls streamed from his nose and surrounded his weathered face. "Ah, you saw your first mermaid, my boy."

"Captain!" Jeremy objected. "Do you think it wise to fill the boy's head with fancies?"

The Captain laughed. "Fancies, Mr. Simmons? You went to sea as a lad a little older than good ol' Jack Quick here, been on the water some six years now, and you think you have seen all there is. I walked a deck since the day I could walk at my father's side, I have seen monsters. Fish the size of a ship that can reduce this boat to driftwood. They surface without warning and send clouds into the skies. And yes, mermaids too. They either come to lead us through a storm safely, or to collect our souls for the devil."

"As to your giant fish, I have heard of them, although I have never seen one myself," Jeremy said, lighting up his pipe, the red glow reflecting the copper streaks in his hair, which was tied tight into a neat ponytail and his equally freshly minted copper eyes lit up brighter as he spoke passionately. "But I have never heard one creditable story of a mermaid. Most are told by those who have had as many years of grog as actual sea duty, and are usually told in exchange for a pint." He laughed. "And they all end with the rum-soaked brain being unable to forget her face, or the love gained and lost in a single glance."

Jack's eyes widened as saucers and glossed over as another wave rocked the Rummy Gale.

The captain squared him up, "a man might well take rum as his mistress once his heart has been touched by a mermaid. Drown himself in drink, as it were, to finish the job left undone by the sea. Jack, my boy, you be too young to feel this now, but I assure thee there be no purer love for a sailor than that for the maidens of the sea."

"You said they come for our souls."

"Well, not all love is reciprocated," claimed the captain.

The boy became unsteady on his feet again, and Jeremy, several inches taller than the Captain was at six-feet caught his arm and steadied him before letting go. "Finish your grog, Jack, then, go below and help me secure our load."

Down in the ship's hold, Jeremy pounded the wooden pegs that held stacks of lumber in place. The beams were four-by-four and twenty-feet in length, stacked floor to ceiling in the lowest of the holds. There were three rows then vertical beams held in place by the pegs, a narrow passage and then the next three rows. The rows ran the length of the Rummy Gale with vertical beams every five-feet. Much more efficient than carrying logs loosely loaded into the ship.

The dark and the grog had Jack's mind playing tricks on him. The waves sounded like knocking, as if someone was desperate to get in; the mallet in Jeremy's hand amplifying the desperation. His hands were smooth but his biceps bulged through his white dress shirt once he removed his blue brass buttoned waistcoat. He was a properly dressed naval man and took pride in keeping his appearance as such while on duty. Jack held the heavy wool coat neatly folded over his arms. "What do you think I saw in the waves, Mr. Simmons, Sir?"

"I do not know, Jack. Maybe the carcass of a dolphin attacked by sharks, but a mermaid… definitely not, my boy." Jeremy pulled on one of the vertical beams. "These are all secure. The Captain was just having a laugh at your expense, and I'm sure he does not believe in mermaids either."

When they returned topside, rain had begun to fall. It was cold and driven by the wind, and the waves were cresting several feet higher. Five bells of the Last Dog Watch, the night was just beginning. Jeremy instructed Jack to return to his cabin off the Captain's quarters, told him to try to sleep, but to stay ready in case he was needed, his words punctuated by a crack of lightning.

Wind and spray tortured the men as they struggled to keep the ship driving through the ever-mounting waves, icy blows sending them tumbling across the deck as waves crashed over the rails. Sails beat louder than thunder as the winds pushed the Rummy Gale where it willed and she leaned dangerously to one side, causing sailors to swing in the riggings. Then she rolled over to the other and the men were tossed back, their bodies striking hard against something in the dark, wave upon wave drenching them in frigid water, sapping their strength.

Each man held to his duty and prayed, some silently, others calling aloud for God's mercies. Jack Roggies held tight to his restraining straps in his hammock, sleep impossible, and thunderclaps as loud as the cannon fire he had heard on his first day aboard.

The Rummy Gale had four cannons on each side, two out the bow and two more pointing aft. His training exercise was to run powder from gun to gun, aft to bow and port to starboard, making sure gunners never ran out of gunpowder and the bags never got wet. Not an easy task as the lower decks always seemed to have a slick film of seawater on them. More importantly, Mr. Simmons informed him, was to stay clear of the gunnery tracks. If he were hit by the recoiling cannon, his injuries could be fatal.

Jack made countless trips from the powder store in the armory with pairs of canvas bags hung around his neck, the fuses connecting the two five-pound bags oily and gritty with black powder, they rubbed his neck raw. The sounds of the cannons made it impossible to hear anything else, so instead of waiting for the gunnery crew to call for more powder, he kept track of how many shots each cannon fired and resupplied them when they were down to their last two.

Both Captain and crew were pleased with his performance and grasp of the situation, and like all other jobs he was assigned to, Jack took to the duties of a powder monkey quickly and naturally.

Right now, however, he would be happy if the boom that rattled his bones was that of cannon fire. But it was not, instead of the flash of cannons, it was the flash from the Almighty. It seemed to be louder than any cannon on the Rummy Gale, and it was aimed at him.

In the darkness, lightning, thunder, howling, and screams all closed in on him. How he wished for the warm glow of his oil lamp, but Mr. Simmons had sternly worded him against the use of such a thing during a storm. "The dark will be terrifying to be sure, but a shattered lamp in your cabin will unleash Hell upon you."

Jack was bawling aloud when Jeremy burst into his cabin, screaming. "On your feet, got to get topside! MOVE lad, there is no time to waste." But the boy was in shock and could not move from his spot. A rush of water propelled Jeremy into the cabin and slammed him against the hammock and he barely managed to get his arms up in time to stop himself from crushing the boy against the wall. Then he gathered him up and sloshed through the calf-deep water.

"What is happening, Mr. Simmons?" asked Jack between sobs. "I'm sorry, but I tried to be a man..."

"You are as much a man as anyone aboard, Mr. Roggies. We are taking on water. The ship is sinking, we must abandon her quickly."

A torrent of seawater rolled over them on the stairs leading to the main deck and a bloodied body thumped against the wall and tumbled down into the darkness. Jack's eyes grew huge at witnessing the spectacle of violence the sea had brought forth. The mizzenmast was broken in two and swung like a pendulum from its riggings, men ensnared in the lines were being whipped about the deck broken and lifeless, and still others hung in the riggings as if a mass execution had been ordered. Jack gripped tighter onto Jeremy's neck. "I don't want to die," he cried.

"You won't, I promise," Jeremy told him sincerely as another massive wave broke over the bow and a surge of frosty sea drove them back. The Rummy Gale, rolling to port, Jeremy climbed along the starboard railing with Jack under his arm.

"Where is Captain Meyers?"

"I am afraid he is gone, swept overboard before I came for you."

A loud crackle above them was followed by their bodies becoming weightless, being flung up, and propelling them through the air. Jeremy gripped the boy tighter, preparing to land he knew not where. He hoped in the water because landing back on deck could kill them both outright, as it had so many of the sailors already.

They were lucky, splashing down in the water surrounded by bits of the Rummy Gale, big and small. The last horrific breaking of wood meaning the ship was doomed. Spotting a part of the mast and yardarm floating nearby, Jeremy swam to it, dragging the unconscious Jack in tow. The sea was surprisingly warmer than he expected and he draped Jack over the cross section. There were a few yards of sail attached to the mast and stretching it out, he tied its corners to the wood.

Jeremy worked quickly to fashion a makeshift raft from the debris, feeling eyes upon him in the darkness. Sharks to be sure, drawn by the trail of bloody bodies already in the water. Rolling Jack onto the sail, he slapped his face a couple of times. He was alive but the ordeal obviously been too much. Jeremy hung onto the raft firmly, as they were tossed around in the angry sea, as it was not big enough to keep both afloat. He could see other items; barrels, pieces of decking, larger too, but he could not risk becoming separated from the boy to swim for one, resigning himself to hold on for as long as he could. This was his charge, his solemn duty, to see this boy safely through the storm and deliver him home.

Home. There was a thought he had clung to in the last few months. This was to be his next to last trip at sea. His duty to the Royal Navy done, he was returning home for Beth, his fiancée, to wed her and bring her to the colonies. Together they would build their future in lumber.

Elizabeth Parisson was a beauty to behold. With bright chestnut eyes peeking out from behind the blackest of lashes, her pink rosy cheeks plumped and caused her obsidian hair to curl around them in a carefree manner. He knew her almost from birth and had watched her grow into the lovely lady she had become and there had hardly been a day that the two had not been found in each other's company. He accompanied her to fetch water from the well; she followed him when he went to chop wood. It was therefore no surprise to either of their families, or townsfolk, when he petitioned her father for her hand.

The war with the French delayed his plans, and being a man of honor, he did not want his wife waiting at home wondering if she were widowed or not. But Jeremy was quick to promise that after his service to the Crown was fulfilled he would return for her. Now that he had his lumber mill running smoothly, he was going to make good on his word. He had faced sword and cannon fire, felt the hot breeze of musket balls sizzling past his face, but they had not altered his plans. So, he was not about to let a little wind and water change them either.

His shipmates' voices became fewer and fewer as the night got darker and longer. He called out periodically, and each time the replies came from farther away. The storm was subsiding but he was exhausted, and he told himself that he had to hold out until dawn, when he could get his bearings and fashion a proper raft for him and the boy. And if he were lucky one of the longboats had survived the sinking and they would be plucked from the sea.

The voices finally went silent in the oppressive darkness and he lost all sensation in his legs. Sporadically, he tried to kick to keep himself warm and alert but they felt like anchors. Then he tasted more blood in the water; not far from him, sharks had claimed yet another shipmate. Jack was safe on the sail but he would draw the predators to them, and as the seas began to calm, his fears were confirmed as they arrived in ever-greater numbers. Mustering his last bit of strength, he kicked hard away and let go of the makeshift raft.

With God's mercy, he might find something he could use to remain afloat not far from the boy. He swam and bobbed around in the water for an eternity but could not see another piece of debris. Then he realized that he could also not see Jack, or any sense in swimming further. He wiped his blurry eyes, not knowing if it was seawater or tears and begged Beth forgiveness as his legs pulled him under.

Instinctively, Jeremy held his breath as he began to sink slowly, but when the burning in his chest grew, he let out tiny air bubbles. Shining like pearls in the shafts of light penetrating the darkness from holes in the sky, he let out the rest of the air in a roiling act of surrender to the inevitable. The fire extinguished, he sank rapidly through the moonbeams.

Chapter 2
A Soul to Save

Eyes about to close, he spotted a shark darting through the rays of light, while several others were still going after his shipmates. He twirled quickly, trying to find it. Damn the beast, he would have his moment of death before becoming its meal. Pulling a dagger from his waist-sash, something struck him from behind, banging hard into his shoulder, and flipped him head over heels. His dagger fell from his grasp and out of sight and the strike dislodged the last air in his lungs. The shark charged.

His eyes widened as the shark changed from fish to female in the alternating bands of light and night. Two hands grabbed his shirt, red tendrils floated about his face, and green emerald eyes locked into his. A powerful fishtail wrapped around his legs and held him taut against her body. Jeremy realized; a mermaid had him, planning to take his soul to the devil. He would not have liked a shark to take his body, he would be damned if he let a mermaid claim his soul. Reaching out, he seized her neck.

In shock, she spun away, flipping him to the surface in a dizzying whirlpool. His head broke the surface for a moment, but only long enough for a single sip of precious air. Falling quickly backwards beneath the waves once more, she was on him again. Locking her arms around his, she pinned them to his side, and with a swish of her tail drove them down into the darkness. He twisted and struggled against her restraint but she held him too tight, and placing her mouth over his, her tongue invaded him.

Just as he was about to lose the battle for his soul, he felt a hot rush of air filling his lungs, penetrating his being with an unknown and peculiar awareness, and renewed energy coursed through his veins like never before. Then as the sensation began to fade, as if he were awakening from a dream, another breath of sweet warm oxygen revived him. She was breathing for him. Her air was exhilarating, imparting a new life force he could not resist taking in. His eyes locked onto hers; his lips to hers; his soul to hers. Her breath not only gave him life-saving oxygen, it calmed and soothed him.

Jeremy no longer struggled to be free, now quite content in her embrace, as she swam effortlessly. Also, unable to tell how fast they were moving or where, he became completely intoxicated by her air. His mind lacking momentary concern for his world, he flew with her in total darkness, lost in time. Sensing neither the flow of water across body nor his body at all, his thoughts focused fully onto her movements, feeling every muscle of her body pressed against his and he loved it.

His body landed hard on a wooden floor, the foul stench of death burning his nostrils. Where was he? Had she taken his soul to the underworld? He groped in the darkness for her, his fingers finding a slime-covered deck and walls. He crawled slowly forward, half expecting to see a pit of fire open before him. There was nothing but the darkness and the cold damp smell of decay.

Hearing a faint tapping not too far from him, he followed it on his hands and knees, but before he could reach it, it stopped and was suddenly replaced by the flickering glow of a candlestick, the small yellow flame pushing back the darkness.

Standing in the dim light with her long crimson hair twisting and curling in every direction, it reached her navel in front and as she turned to place the single candle on the mantle behind her, the silky strands curled upward at the small of her back. It was thick, hiding most of her face as she looked down, and cloaking her upper body in a waterfall of flames. Then gazing towards him, he noticed that her skin was unblemished and smooth, the complexion of Egyptian alabaster. Candlelight shimmered and danced along her cheeks, and on the dark cherry ruby lips, which were plump, soft, and moist. Her eyes appeared like fire trapped within emerald irises, with pupils of lighthouse beacons. She was splendidly put-together, with long arms and legs, her small breasts completely hidden beneath all the hair and the small round hips of a young woman in her early twenties. She moved with mesmeric precision through the cabin, floating more than walking on her small bare feet. He had never seen a woman in this state of undress before, never seen a woman possessing such elegant beauty. Now he was sure that he had drowned.

She stood beside the dancing tongue of fire and he looked up at the pair of glowing emeralds that stared knowingly at him. So, was this Heaven, or was he in Hell? Was she an angel here to guide him through eternity? Or, was she his tormentor? He wondered, but whichever it was, it made no difference; he would gladly be with her forever.

This is the Sea Queen, her thoughts invaded his mind, *and you are not dead. I rescued you from the storm and brought you here.*

"So, you have a ship. That is great. How many did you rescue? And where is Jack? Were you able to save the boy?"

He has you to thank for being alive. Here, is only you.

"How can that be? Alert your men, we may still be able to rescue some of the others."

There are no men. The Sea Queen rests on the bottom.

Jeremy ran past her, down the gangway, and threw himself against the cabin door. It resisted him with a solid thud. He struggled against it, driving with his legs through his shoulder but the portal was steadfast and immovable. He returned to the cabin and sank into a chair, casting his eyes down, avoiding her, "why did you bring me here?"

I had no place else to take you, we are too far from land. She noticed his gaze wandering about the cabin, as he shivered violently.

Clutching his hands before his face, he breathed a heavy cloud on them.

What is wrong? Have I offended you?

"No. You have not," Jeremy said shamefaced, "it is that you are unclothed, so I should not be looking at you. And I am freezing."

You are wet and need to put on dry clothes to keep warm. And if it pleases you, I shall put on some too. Come with me.

She led him through the ship aft and up into what he imagined was the Captain's quarters. Along the way, he passed a corpse, long mummified by the frigid temperatures. There, he found several chests. Pulling clothes out that smelled of old age, he quickly changed out of his wet ones.

Jeremy sensed Shera's eyes on him but when he turned, she had already disappeared. Now, how did he know her name, as she had never mentioned it? Searching through the Captain's quarters for some clue as to what had taken place there, he realized that she had never spoken at all, yet he was filled with the feeling of knowing her since the first moment. Perhaps this was a fever dream. The shipwreck, his drowning, this mermaid Shera, it was all unreal anyway. Exhausted, he extinguished the lone candle and crawled into the bed.

Jeremy awoke alone in unfamiliar surroundings and it took a few minutes for his mind to recall the events of the previous day. Poor Jack Quick, he thought. His mother had lost a husband and now her eldest son. So, what had God in store for him? Was he to be likened to Jonah in the belly of the great fish? If so, what sins had he to atone for?

He could tell from the garbs he was wearing that the ship had been on the bottom for a long time. Unearthing the Captain's journal, he turned quickly to the last entry of the ship's log. It was dated April 5th 1585 in the year of our Lord.

Davin Cutter, eight bells of the morning watch, the storm has come upon us straight from Hell. There was no sunrise, and a foul wind lashes at the riggings. Men, who went aloft, were torn from the yardarms and were lost to the deep. The topsails and topgallants are gone in whole and the main sails will be soon. The sea has sent forth pounding waves determined to break us at the beam. God forgive me for taking the Witch Rehema into this old fool's house.

Jeremy reckoned the ship had been on the bottom close to two hundred years, so he explored his underwater prison and discovered that he could go down another two decks on the Brigantine vessel before finding water and could also make his way from bow to stern on either deck. He surmised she had gone down in one piece, perhaps taking water over the side and capsizing, unlike the Rummy Gale. The last he had seen of his ship had been when her stern broke away at a right angle from a wave hitting it at the midsection and they had been whipped through the air and into the sea.

Naturally, he could not open any hatch leading topside but there had to be a way out of the ship given that Shera had brought him to this great pocket of air trapped in the middle. Somewhere in the below flooded decks there must exist an open portal. At the ship's stern, back in the Captain's quarters, the windows had grown bright for a time and he could make out shadows on the stained glass. Huge fish, he imagined, patrolling the wreck, although any food to be had must have been exhausted already. He found his way to the galley, but anything that had once been edible had long since petrified.

Why had Shera brought him to this graveyard? Did she have a plan in mind for him? Where had she gone? He searched the ship from end to end, looked in every store, found black powder and shots, sails, lines, sheets, and halyards, and tools in good order. He broke into one locked store and discovered the ship's rum supply. The sun had to be above the yardarm by now, he reckoned, so he took a good long drink, to quench his thirst, to silence the hunger, and to make sense of his impossible situation. He searched the whole of the Sea Queen. The years under water had treated her well. She was solid on the inside and he imagined she was likewise all the way through. Solid, silent, and in solitude. As was he, Shera was no longer onboard.

From the lightening and darkening of the windows in the Captain's quarters, he counted three days passing. He could not tell if the ship was still facing east but from

Cutter's logs, the Sea Queen had put to sea from New Amsterdam and was travelling southeast to the Islands to pick up a cargo of rum before heading across the ocean to Falmouth, England. The rum and log made passing time a little easier to bear, as Jeremy followed the story closely. They had been on the seventh day of their voyage when they ran into the storm that sent her to the bottom. She had been at sea longer than the Rummy Gale when it sank, but probably still closer to the American coast. He studied her charts and tried to decipher how far out to sea he was presently, for if Shera's intentions were to save his life, he would have to find his own way home, which meant he would have to know where he was now.

Falmouth. There was a place and life Jeremy did not miss. The Janus was anchored a mile offshore and the smell and gray cloud still enveloped them in its sinfulness. This was their last stop before heading to the New World to engage the French. Odd, he thought, they sailed west across an endless ocean to engage an enemy that was just across a Channel.

Falmouth was a navy town in every way. From the foundries and shipyards belching smoke into the skies, to drunken sailors passed out in the streets around the taverns. For Jeremy, this had been the first time he had seen women so scantily attired, as there had not been this kind of life in Shanklin, on the Isle of Wight in the north east.

He had been sent with two other junior officers to procure supplies for the men. As explained to him in the longboats going to shore, "'tis not the task of a man with brass on his uniform."

"Why not give the men leave? They can do as they wish until morning." He asked curiously the mates in his boat, not understanding the logic completely.

"It would be infinitely harder to get the men back onboard than to get the women off in the morning. Giving that these men will not touch shore again for some years, if ever. A petticoat liberty is a service more than a kindness. As a midshipman, you are entitled to a sampling before they are brought back to the ship," informed another midshipman two years his senior, "and no one will begrudge you taking a favorite for yourself."

He then understood the need for two more longboats in tow. The three men went from tavern to piss-smelly tavern along the wharf looking for women who were not too past their prime. Some of the women were as worn down and washed out as the structures they leaned against and he was not entirely sure which was holding up which. Jeremy had no knowledge of such affairs so he let his two companions strike the deals and conduct the interviews. And they delighted in his discomfort in the matter, nudging him saying, "What of the pair on this one? She can feed a lot, ye thinks?"

Jeremy simply dropped his eyes to the ground, declaring, "you know I am betrothed."

One young woman, probably about the same age as Beth, with bright and curly blonde shoulder length hair stepped up to him, "I'll wager your special lady would benefit from the experience I can provide you. Most men find it helpful to know what to do before their wedding night. And she is expecting you to know how she should be handled as a woman."

"Yes, this is true, my friend. We will take her too. And if Mr. Simmons is too shy to make use of such a fine specimen, I assure you that I am not."

Four of the women left the tavern with them: the big bosomed one, the curly blonde, and two others of ample proportions and age. Then they continued on to another place where women congregated around the door. That time, Jeremy remained outside with the four 'purchases'. The well-endowed woman explaining that it could become problematic if they were to enter another's establishment.

It took a while for his companions to emerge from the tavern and Mary, the curly blonde, told Jeremy, "without you dampening the process, they are doubtless having a proper sampling of what there is on offer to your men. This is a first-rate house, it is."

"You know the ladies who work here?" asked Jeremy.

"Indeed," she replied cheerfully, "me mum does." After registering the queer look from him, she added defensively, "we can't all take in stitching and the wash, you know. But we all have to eat."

24

"I suppose." Jeremy said, realizing how judgmental he appeared. "Why do you not work here then?"

"A bit odd, wouldn't it be? I mean, one night you are servicing some jack, then the next night it's your mum's turn. No, it's best not to know."

The other women laughed heartily and Jeremy felt even more squeamish. And a few minutes later he was very glad to see the pair of sailors finally reappear with six more ladies in tow, and rather broad smiles. "Good, you are back. Are we done with this business then?"

"Patience, my boy, we are just getting started. And remember, we have three boats to fill. Besides, there are over a hundred men onboard, you don't want to see these precious flowers plucked to the stem, do you?"

A new woman to the group, older than his mom, grabbed his arm and wrapped it in hers. "Ah, first petticoat roundup. You must be James; your mates spoke highly of you."

He let the mistake in his name slip as she smelt of whiskey and was using him mostly as a crutch. They continued for the rest of the afternoon and into the early evening. At times, Jeremy was sent in to do the examinations and make the purchases. He was none too happy about it and never did more than pick the cleanest of the women from the lineup provided.

Finally, they loaded the longboats with thirty-six women, not necessarily evenly divided, and each sailor and three of the women rowed out to the Janus. The men lined the deck as the boats approached, cheering wildly.

One of the other midshipmen yelled across to Jeremy, "and you would deny these brave men this last chance of civilized life."

Jeremy shouted back, "I don't believe they are or will be so civil once they are on board."

He watched the women climb the boarding ladders to the first row of gun ports with no problems. Obviously, this was not their first petticoat liberty. Next, he passed through the crew quarters where several of the hammocks had been taken down and curtains strung up to section off areas, cots lined up between the curtains for more suitable bedding, which were immediately being put to use. When he reached the weather deck, music was being played and rum liberally poured. Then he noticed that his fellow midshipmen were the highest-ranking members of the crew onboard, which meant there were no officers left aboard. The ship belonged to the crew for the night.

The Captain watched through his telescope as the three longboats cut over the silver surface like arrows as they approached the Janus. When he saw Jeremy and the others halfway to the ship, he, his lieutenants and accompanied by the ship's warrant officers launched their own longboats and headed for shore. Naturally, it would not have been proper for the captain to be present while the ship received supplies such as those due to arrive.

Although the midshipmen were the highest-ranking officers left in charge, the captain had also left the Boatswain and the Master-at-arms to make sure they maintained order. He did not worry about men jumping ship; after all, only a fool would do so tonight.

Their boats docked just in time to hear cheers ring out from the Janus, the officers quick to take carriages to their favorite boarding houses in town, which, the further away from the docks the nicer they became, the streets clean and quiet, the walls well looked after with fresh coats of paint every year, and vestibules brightly lit and welcoming. Near the town square were a few blocks of houses where a gentleman could get a good meal, smoke a pipe, engage in conversation with fellow seamen of rank over decent bourbon, and at the end of the night, retire upstairs to a clean bed with a scented cocotte. But although well-dressed and good-looking, the women were never seen in the parlor downstairs, remaining in the sitting rooms upstairs where the men would choose whom to take to bed with them.

The captain and his lieutenants took a carriage up a road leading out of town, heading towards Kennington Manor, an estate owned by Lord Kennington, proprietor of a foundry and shipyard. A good and loyal friend of the captain, Lord Kennington had christened the Janus himself. It was the only ship the captain commanded in his distinguished career.

The new arrivals were treated to a lavish dinner with other captains and officers, whose ships would also soon depart for the colonies, then enjoyed parlor music by ladies in white lace and satin dresses. Spoke of war and battle plans, and debated the troubles rising in the west with their host and his courtesans. The ladies the very picture of upper class society, well groomed, highly educated, and extremely skilled at making a man forget his wife and family for the duration.

They would spend the better part of the week at the Manor while Jeremy returned the women to shore the next day and the men of the Janus made her ready for sea. On the captain's return the Janus would set sail for the colonies immediately.

Chapter 3
No Reprieve

Shera opened a hatch in the floor of the crew's quarters
that led to the oars gangway on the starboard side, then
stepped in the hole and let the lid drop behind her. Jeremy
Simmons was fixated on the young boy tied to the raft, so
she had clouded his mind with sounds of wind and
thunder, and blinded his eyes with flashes of fire from the
sky. He did not hear her leave, did not notice he was alone
with his thoughts, tortured as he was with feelings of loss
and regret, which led to remorse and recriminations. But
she would ease his pain, and make certain the boy, Jack
Quick, survived the night.

The water energized her instantly and the leg muscles relaxed and unfolded, fanned out from her inner thighs down, joined in the front and back then thinned and spread until her feet became flippers. Her tail was thick and powerful; the bones having stretched and softened to the consistency of cartilage, allowing it to twist and turn, as she propelled herself to the boy. The transformation took place at the same time as her lungs filled with water that effervesced to air, a mere blink of an eye, or a sneeze. The air kept her buoyant, allowing her to swim faster and a single swish jetted her through the gaping hole in the side of the ship.

She forced herself as fast as she could back into the stormy sea; each swing of her tail equivalent to a hundred oars on a ship. As long as Jeremy kept his mind on Jack Quick, she could feel his presence, sense where he was, and be guided to him. Soon, she was back where the Rummy Gale had sunk, the smell of blood in the water burning her nostrils, the same scent that called to the sharks. Dozens had already arrived. More would be on their way.

Ordinarily, she had nothing to fear from the sharks. She was faster and stronger than even the great whites, and she could dissuade them with her mind, but this was a feeding frenzy. They charged, mouth agape, ready to swallow whatever they encountered.

Resolute, she caught up with Jack on the makeshift raft. He stirred as she grabbed the mast carefully from below, so as not to reveal herself. Presently, she discovered that the rig was being pushed further out to sea on the warm flow, making it cumbersome and awkward to steer out of the currents.

Jack awoke to the burning sun beating on his back, the vast ocean all he could see. Glints of light bounced off the crests of the waves, painfully striking his eyes, which quickly filled with tears as he thought of his newly made friends and their loss, also knowing that he would never see his Virginian farm again. Alone and despondent, he looked to the cool ocean, the calm beckoning invitingly to join his friends below the waves. Because, why should he live when all the others had given their lives, especially Mr. Jeremy Simmons, who had saved his.

About to roll over the edge of the sail, he spotted a sea fire beneath his raft. Surely, this was a school of fish, as it was too fluid to be a solid object, or perhaps, it was a piece of cloth snagged by the rigging when the Rummy Gale had gone down.

Jack reached down and let the crimson run through his fingers, immediately being reminded of the finest strands of his mother's hair, which he had played with in his boyhood. Rolling the silken streams between his fingers, he longed for his mother's soothing voice. Despair gripping him deeply and without thinking, he yanked the red mass from the sea.

Shock and fear replaced dark thoughts of death and drowning, the hair was attached to a woman's head. At least that was what he imagined seeing in the splash of water, but perhaps it had been a sprite. Then, a tail slapped him across the face, as the shark leapt over the raft, tossing him into the sea.

Struggling to climb back onto the sail, he coughed and spat brine back into the sea instinctively and rolled the makeshift craft in the waves, panic-stricken by the thought of the shark's return. Finally managing to clamber back onto the raft and stabilizing himself again, he would swear he had felt hands lift him out of the water. He believed they were hands, as he was sure he had felt gentle fingers on his back and legs. But as he looked around searchingly, he knew there was no one who could have given him aid. There was nothing, no person, no shark, no red-haired lady, just the endless blue sea. Hours later, he began puzzling over something that had been bothering him the entire day, and was only now starting to make sense; in a way. He had been drifting systematically against the current.

Shera had taken hold of the rigging dangling below the raft and pulled Jack along at a safe distance from hands and eyes. On she swam but after two days, they were still far from shore. She was not necessarily trying to take the boy all the way to land, but rather hoping to find a ship that would spot him and rescue him. However, the seas were quiet this time of year.

Most ships that headed east had started their journey two moons past. The boy's ship, Jeremy Simmons' ship, the Rummy Gale, was very late in her journey and that had been what had drawn her attention first, and when they turned east instead of continuing south, she had known that all were in grave danger. She had also felt something in Jeremy, not quite desperation, more a sense of urgency. She knew he had to make the voyage, although, it was unclear why. Perhaps, it had to do with Jack. They were not related but she felt a protective intensity when he thought about the boy, and she had felt it deep and strong before the storm. Even now, his thoughts burnt like sun metal on her skin, so she had to get this boy to safety, even if it meant swimming all the way to shore.

It was another two days before Shera heard the sound of nets in the water a distance away. Towing the boy as close as she dared before leaving him in their path, she then heard a man cry out, "Avast, mates, man overboard off the port bow."

Satisfied, she returned to the deep, exhausted, but unable to stop for a rest, as Jeremy needed saving too. With her strength sapped, she needed help, needed in fact to get to the Winter Seas. But that meant another six-hundred-mile swim. She would never reach it alone. There was only one way.

She called out to a pod of whales a few miles away and got a ride on one of them, a common practice of maidens who travelled long distances. She merely looked into the eye of a five-year-old female and the animal understood immediately what was required. Shera lay on her back, her fingertips adhered to the skin near the dorsal fin, where she would not disturb the young whale. She recalled the day this beautiful creature had been born; her mother had had a difficult time pushing her out. All the maidens had gathered around imparting their energies to aid the birth. The newborn calf had sunk like a rock at first, but then a spark of life took hold and she swam up against her mother. There had been great joy in the Winter Seas that day. The young whale swam out ahead of the pod. They would be there in two days.

Shera arrived in the shallow waters just north of the equator, the many islands there drawing men and maidens alike for the cold months. The weather was warm and the waters calm, the last of the storms finally having passed through, leaving a trail of destruction on land and in the sea. Many of the islanders had drowned in the floodwaters and on ships that had been sunk, including the Rummy Gale when the storm had caught her in its death grip.

The storm had claimed maidens' lives too; dozens of her sisters had been slammed against rocks by the powerful waves. Tempests often battered many of their underwater sanctuaries near the shores; this one had been no different. The Winter Seas' waters tasted of blood, sharks were plentiful, these waters were dangerous.

Shera swam into the mouth of Usea Maya, the entrance to their undersea kingdom, carefully scanning the columns and spikes rising from the floor and dropping from the ceiling as a precaution against sharks lurking in the dwindling light.

Although she would hear its breathing before she could see it, the echoes from the cavern walls made it dangerous and a fully-grown great white could easily be waiting behind a shimmering crystal column. The main cavern had a myriad of other caves, which honeycombed beneath the island. Some led to dead ends, very dead ends, as sharks, barracudas, and moray eels made them their homes.

But Shera had swum these corridors thousands of times in her three hundred years and could navigate them backwards with her eyes closed. Turning left, she went deeper under the mountain. There, she relaxed; no predator ventured down this far from the open sea. Crabs, shrimp, and mussels were all one found in these caves.

There was no surface light in here either, the sharp walls the only peril she faced now. Brushing against a jagged rock or a protruding spur would be a costly mistake, ripping her open from head to tail before she knew what she had done. The barbs were not a natural occurrence in the rock, but instead, chiseled over centuries as defenses, as the Maiden realm had splintered and reformed many times. Shera had not been through here in two decades, choosing to live outside the Queen's domain.

Approaching maturity, Shera had found herself at odds with regulations and restrictions. Headstrong and outspoken, she found it difficult to remain within the territorial waters, instead choosing the open seas to the north, only returning to the area in winter, rarely visited Usea Maya, and selected to make her home on one of the coral reefs that dotted the area.

She was not alone in her way of thinking, as quite a few other maidens formed small communities outside the realm, some even encouraging her to join them, but Shera preferred solitude. Those who lived in the colder climates, like her, only returned to the Winter Seas and Usea Maya when the waters became frigid. Most were much older, as maidens of her age were usually not permitted to venture far, as Rehema commanded. She had elected to ignore the ruling, much to the Queen's annoyance, which immediately put her on the wrong footing for what she had come for this day.

A tiny shimmering circle of turquoise and azure appeared above her head. Two flicks of her tail and the circle expanded rapidly as she rocketed to the surface, a hundred feet per second and she burst from the pool in a rainbow shower, her body expelling the life-sustaining seawater from every pore. Her tail split from the center of her fins and shriveled up her body. Her bones contracted, thickened, and hardened into two sturdy legs. Her fins shrank to a fraction of their size to give her a pair of petite feet to land upon and she touched down gracefully on the soft mossy carpet inside the cave.

Bird songs and fragrant flowers filled the towering mountain cradle. Sunlight sprinkled down, reflecting off the minerals in the rock walls, the island alive with color and sounds of paradise, and her mind rang with the thoughts of hundreds of her kind greeting and welcoming her back home. Maidens began appearing in the pools and aqueducts leading to the various chambers inside their mountain home, most remaining in true form, sitting alongside the waterways beating their tails on the surface. The cavern filling to ear-splitting levels from the commotion.

Some leapt and others walked from the sea transforming into their bipedal forms before they left the water, gathering around her, exchanging a three-figure touch to her forehead. Shera folded the thumb and pinky of her left hand to her palm and lightly touched their foreheads in response, her index and ring finger above the eyes and her middle finger resting a moment in the center, sharing The Knowing.

Usea Maya was an unnoticeable island on the surface, a green and black dot in an ocean of blue, which was barely a mile long and half as wide. To one side, a small forest existed, with a good sprinkling of azure pools. But the rest was mostly brush, grass, and moss that covered the exposed stony surface, their roots wedged into the cracks in the black volcanic rock. Its peak was not high enough to keep the waves out in a strong wind, so there was a constant rainfall of seawater into the caldera of the old volcano.

However, below the surface, Usea Maya was formidable, sinking 24,680 feet to the ocean floor, its base 51,200 feet across, with many cracks, fissures, and vents along its gentle slopes. Usea Maya was dormant, but not a dead volcano and its heat was felt throughout the black crystalline chambers. There were many rooms, some large, but none as great or grand as the Throne Room, which was in the center of the mountain.

A huge waterfall hundreds of feet high dominated the cavern, the water thundering down the wall opposite the entrance where Shera stood. It cascaded onto a ledge filling a basin where Rehema, the Queen, sat on her curled tail. The water spilled into two streams filling shallow pools before continuing down the rock face. The Queen's ministers and advisors occupied those pools.

Throughout the cavern smaller waterfalls poured into pools on ledges along the walls where maidens gathered. Usea Maya, as it had been told to Shera, was the first Volcano. It was here that the oceans of the world had sprung forth as steam billowing into the sky, raining down in an unending deluge, and now the water returned to its origin to replenish the Earth under the mountain. The walls and floor of this huge chamber still glowed red hot in places, and there were steam vents producing white whispery veils, the two effects combining to light the place in a warm and dim atmosphere.

Shera stood in the middle of the hall accompanied by her sisters, all older than herself by a few hundred years, and her aunts, older still, a hazy vapor enshrouding them all to their knees. She hated this place; it was like standing in a thunderstorm. The Queen was barely visible a distance away in the mist.

Why have you come to me like this?

I come seeking aid, to ask for...

I know what you seek. The Queen's thought silenced her mind. *And why do you appear before me in this inferior form?*

38

I spend so much time in my natural shape; it is nice to stretch my legs. Shera joked.

The chamber was flooded with thoughts condemning, supporting, and excusing hers as the immaturity of her youth. The Queen silenced them all.

You think you have saved this man's life. You have not. You merely delayed the eventuality of his death. The sailor has gone to sea and the sea has claimed him. We do not interfere.

That is not true. Many others have rescued men from the waters.

Yes, but without exposing themselves. If your Jeremy Simmons was to survive now, he would forever search for you, for us, hunt us down and kill us all. Or do worse.

Shera's anger was unmasked in her body and mind. *You know he has a good heart. Unblemished and true is he. I have touched his heart and I cannot leave him to die. He saved the boy and sacrificed his own wellbeing doing so.*

Shera, you are young, and have not experienced the world of men. When facing their own demise, they will do great acts in the hope of clearing away their sins. Given time, he will become a killer, as all men are. And it will be you he will seek to destroy. You cannot make a pet of a shark. And you cannot make friends with a man.

Shahira, Shera's older sister by a century, stepped forward. She was an oddity even among maidens, her inky black hair shorter and straight, with a coal-like skin that glowed and reflected the fire from within the volcanic rock. And like Usea Maya, she was tall and strong, with

39

powerful legs, and arms like a man's, and to complete the picture of anomaly, she had eyes like the sky.

I am not as young as my sister and I have been on the surface world, whereas she has not. I have also discovered that some men are good sometimes and some men are bad sometimes. No man, or for that matter maiden, is all of one and none of the other. And I have heard told, of times long gone by when Man and Maiden worked together. Therefore, I will aid Shera in her efforts to save this one.

Rehema sprung from her perch, dove into the deep crevice before her and emerged from the heated water in human form, making her way to the women. Placing her three fingers to Shera's forehead, she transformed her against her will. A blatant show of power that was not lost to any, as Shera writhed at her feet.

See the dissent you have brought to this chamber, child? Yes, there was a time maiden and man existed in unison but men have become corrupted with conquest and hoarding the bounty of this world. Greed and the lust for power will cloud the mind of even the most honorable among them. Their craving for sun and moon metals drives them out of their minds. This I know, for I have seen it. The world of men is dangerous, they have abandoned God, and God has abandoned them. Stay away from them. This goes for all of you. And diving back into a nearby pool, she disappeared into the maze.

Shera sat and curled her tail shamefully around her body, tears streaming down her face as much from anger as the humiliation she felt.

Thoughts cascaded down from the other maidens as loud as the water from the falls.

Shreya, Shera's eldest sister knelt beside her and transformed. A beautiful five-hundred-year-old mermaid, she had a coppery tone in her skin that mirrored the tawny sparkle of her eyes, and her thick brunette hair was braided into ropes hanging around her body, sweeping the floor at her feet. Then she and Shahira wrapped their younger sister in their tails from either side. Each placing three fingers to her temples, they blocked out the angry thoughts.

Slowly, the chamber cleared.

Those in support of the young maiden's request quietly went away in the running waters of their pools, but those who followed their queen, made a show of disapproval, diving from their perches into the various canals running through the chamber, making loud splashes and beating their tails against the water as if wagging fingers at the naughty girl. After a while, the place became empty, except for the trio of young maidens.

Shera spent the next night on a nearby island called The Turks, in Cockburn Town, the streets littered with drunken pirates, most of whom, were stranded by the storms. Shahira had given her a red and white linen dress to wear. Shera had been onshore in the past, but usually avoided crowded places, mainly staying near deserted coves and empty beaches. She had probably only met half a dozen men in her three hundred years but this was different, she needed to acquire food for Jeremy. Shera felt the pain of his hunger and she ached too.

There was only one place open for business, the Iron Rostrum, and from the tales of her sister, it was a rum house, a place where men drank and slept, and food could be purchased. She would not need rum, as she already knew that Jeremy had found the ship's supply. She passed by the men undetected until she reached the bar.

A very old and very fat man said, "M'Lady, what brings you to a scuttlebutt like this at such an hour?"

I be in need of food and supplies for a man, and a watertight jack-joint to carry it all.

"A watertight bag, M'Lady," the large barkeep looked quizzically at her, "ah, you plan to swim to your Jack."

Yes, I am, and it is a long way, so it must be sturdy.

The man returned a while later with several tins of meat sealed with wax, a loaf of bread wetted and rolled in heavy salt, then wrapped in cloth and again in leather. Several large jars of rice, sugar cane, dry beans, and placed it all in a large gunnysack, which he tarred the outside of then wrapped the whole order in a small fishing net and tied the top.

Shera dumped two small gold coins on the bar from the purse on a string she carried.

As she left the tavern, the keeper said to the man staring into his pint of ale, "Isn't that the strangest thing

42

you ever saw? A little wisp of a woman carrying all that stuff, said she is going to swim out to her man."

"What woman?" Asked the drunken sailor.

Shera stood on the beach in the moonlight, waves washing over her feet, seeing Jeremy stumbling about the Sea Queen, rum and hunger gnawing at his mind. It had been more than a week since the ship wrecked and he was in a fit, questioning his reality, her nature, the very fabric of life. But what weighed heaviest on his mind was Jack Quick's fate, the boy he had promised a mother to protect.

She waded further into the water, her dress billowing up with the incoming tide then untying the white ribbon down the front, she pulled the garment over her head. Advancing into the surf with the dress and fishnet of supplies in hand, a wave washed over her and plastered her hair to her breasts. Momentarily motionless, she drew strength from the power of the waves. Her mind expanded, carried on the tides, suffered Jeremy's pain strong and deep in her stomach then sensed the warmth of Jack's safety but frightened aboard the fishing ship. She reached out further still, her mind like the moonlight across the water, touching the Captain, who abruptly changed course for the Chesapeake Bay and young Jack Roggies immediately felt tranquility wash over him. Jeremy too relaxed, knowing the boy was safe, then seeing her standing in the sea, enticing him to feel the comfort of her body, he finally fell asleep in her tender embrace.

She folded the dress into the fishnet and slung it across her back. There were over a thousand miles ahead of her but Jeremy would sleep while she swam. She was determined, energized and rejuvenated, and certain that she would make the journey back to the Sea Queen before the moon rose again. Lying out, she flicked her tail; gone from Cockburn Town, miles away from The Turks, catching the warm current north.

Jeremy stirred, his mind struggling to find its way back to his body. His legs, arms, back and stomach, the pain ricocheting through him at that last thought. Falling from the bed to his knees, he heaved vehemently, the lack of food making it a futile effort. He fumbled in the darkness for the bottle, found it, then just as quickly lost interest. She was back.

He had found the hatch to the oars deck days ago, so grabbing a lantern, he went there. Jumping down the hole, he held up the light. Shera rose halfway out of the water and tossed the fishnet of food to him. He clawed at it and the large loaf of bread broke in half. Stuffing fistfuls into his mouth, he chewed fast and swallowed hard.

Resting on her arms, Shera watched contently as Jeremy ate nearly half of the rations she had brought. Eventually, he slowed down and she could see he was starting to feel sick from all he had consumed then without warning he slid down against the wall and looked deep into her eyes crazily. She shrank away.

"No. Please don't go!" Jeremy cried out. "You are real. And I'm not dead. Or am I?"

I am real and I told you already that you are very much alive. But fear not, I will not leave you here.

"So, you are a mermaid," Jeremy giggled and shook his head.

We are maidens. You know me as Shera.

"Why do I hear you inside my head?"

This is the way we communicate. I went to get help but none is coming. Hand me my dress.

"Oh, yes, of course. Here you go." Jeremy held out the bundle of wet clothes. "Forgive me, but you are the most beautiful of God's creations."

Shera lifted herself out of the water and the transformation began and ended in a few seconds. Jeremy was amazed, sure he had seen a tail but it was gone and a full woman stood before him, naked and wet.

Be not concerned, I am not cold. The dress is for your comfort; my body is quite used to the temperature. We will be here for a while, waiting for a passing ship.

After Shera slipped the dress over her head and did up the laces, they returned to the Captain's quarters. They spent days and nights probing each other's minds, making discoveries about each other's characters and lives. Winter was setting in but neither articulated what the other felt. No ship would be passing nearby any time soon. They would have to find another way to shore.

Chapter 4
The Price of Love

Jeremy taught Shera how to use her voice. She, of course, knew all the words but had no practice in uttering them. Jeremy was the first man she had met who was alive, outside the barkeeper the night before. All the other sailors she had encountered before were drowning, mere moments from death. She had brought them solace in their final seconds, as maidens had done throughout the ages.

"Perhaps, that is why men have come to fear the sight of maidens at sea," Shera said slowly and deliberately. "But some think of us as saviors, as did your Captain."

"You knew the Captain?" Jeremy enquired.

"Yes, I met him as a boy. He lost his father and brother to pirates," Shera recalled, "he escaped by jumping into the sea. I took him to shore." Her eyes darkened and Jeremy felt the sadness overtake her. "I am sorry I could not save him this time. But I did bring him peace before his passing on. He was happy to see me again."

Jeremy pondered her statements. How could she know him as a boy? Taking the Captain's age into consideration, that had to have taken place more than fifty years previously, but she could not be more than a young woman herself, probably around twenty years old, no more, from the looks of her.

Shera realized what he must be thinking from the puzzled look he acquired. She had stopped invading his mind, wanting to give him the privacy of his own thoughts. And it was also dangerous now as the Queen had forbidden her to aid him. She was blocking herself from her sisters but the Queen was powerful. Rehema could enter one's mind no matter how hard one resisted, and if aided by her court, no secret would stay hidden for long.

Shera informed him. "Yes, I am a young woman by your understanding."

Jeremy glanced at her again, recalling the way she had looked the first time he had seen her without clothes.

However old she was, he should be so lucky to look that good in ten years. He should be so well in a month, he thought.

Shera left at intervals for a few days at a time to get more provisions. But this time when she returned, she noticed Jeremy had weakened significantly. She asked if the food was not enough.

Sadly, he told her, "it is not the food. I'm afraid the air within these walls grows foul. If we do not get out of here soon, I don't think I will survive."

She nodded. "Aye, I taste it too. My fastest swim to the nearest land is a little over two days but we will have to make a try for it anyway. There is nothing along the shore for hundreds of miles but it is where I am gathering berries and nuts for you."

"It will have to do," agreed Jeremy.

"There is one more thing you must be aware of," Shera warned, "to gain the greatest speed I must swim submerged and I will breathe for the both of us."

"This is a problem for you, isn't it?"

"It will sap my strength. If I become too weak, we will both drown."

Jeremy was quick to decide, "then you cannot take the chance. There is no sense in both of us dying. Besides, you gave me more days than I deserved."

Shera's temper flared up, "don't be so quick to give up your life, Jeremy Simmons. It was noble to save the boy, it is foolish to sit here and die. We will try."

Jeremy refused to go, and they argued over it for the next couple of days. He suggested Shera try to find a passing ship, as she had done for Jack. She agreed and each day she swam around looking for something, and each day she returned with bad news. This being the winter season, no ships ventured so far from land. Any shipping to be found would be along the coast between the cities of the north, New York, Boston, and New Haven.

Then they decided to start going to the surface for fresh air daily, both floating in the sunshine for hours. Sometimes, she transformed and other times, she went in human body. She knew he preferred her human form, as he breathed easier with her like that. It made her sad.

Jeremy had not realized how gloomy it had become within the sunken vessel, as eyesight adapts, or how much he missed the sun, even when it pierced his eyes like daggers. But he enjoyed sharing air with Shera on their trips to and from the Sea Queen so much more, enjoyed it so much, he often regretted reaching the surface, or returning to the ship. Thoughts of going home, of Beth, and their intended marriage had completely vanished from his mind. He was beginning to wish that he could remain undersea locked in their embrace, also knowing that Shera felt it too, as their trips had started taking longer each day.

One day on the surface, he told her, "the air below is hardly breathable anymore."

Shera agreed then announced as she gazed into the distance. "There is a storm on the horizon. It will be upon us within a day or two. We may have to make an attempt to reach shore before then."

"We shall leave tonight."

They floated in the cool sunshine, each locked in their own thoughts. Then feeling Jeremy reach out to her, she opened her mind to his thoughts for the first time in weeks.

You must promise me that if you have to, you will let me go. I cannot be responsible...

It will not come to that. And if we cannot make it, I will turn back before it is too late.

Jeremy squeezed her hand. *Take your natural form. It does not disturb me as you think, not as much as your human form does.*

Shera smiled and wrapped her tail around him and as they sank into the water and locked lips there was less an exchange of air and more an exploration of each other. Her tail faded back to legs and she wrapped them around his. They sank quicker, lost in their embrace then swam through the hole in the port side. Jeremy stopped in the opening and stretched his arms from side to side then reaching up to the top he counted six broken boards on the side of the ship. The break was below the oar ports, but maybe not quite below the sea line.

Shera returned from one last search for a ship. She had
only been gone an hour but it was long enough to know
that they would have to swim the entire distance to shore.
She did not have to see a ship as she swam around, she
listened for the sounds of the hull cutting through the
waves. She had neither heard nor seen a ship in a moon,
they were all alone.

She did however hear the approaching storm and
knew it was time. She stepped off the oar deck and
transformed. In her natural form, she was almost twice
Jeremy's body length, as her tail from hip to fin was seven
feet. Jeremy carried their clothes in a net strapped to his
back. It was more efficient for them to swim naked and
her soft breasts warmed his chest against the icy ocean
that constantly stung his arms and legs. Jeremy could only
take a few hours on the surface lately and his return to the
Sea Queen was followed by hours under the heavy quilting
on board. Shera knew her swimming would at least
generate a great deal of body heat, as it was how she too
withstood the frigid temperatures of the winter waters,
although, by this time, alone, she would have been much
further south. She hoped now that she could generate
enough heat for the both of them.

Locked together by the mouth, his legs wrapped
around her hips, and her arms cradling his body to her, she
swished her tail and off they went. Ever vigilant for signs of
sharks, she swam at a steady pace, her eyes glowing
emerald green as she scouted for the predators. She
fought the urge to push herself at top speed, as doing so
would make her breathing so rapid the pressure would

rupture Jeremy's lungs. Everything she did, she did for two.

Jeremy tasted the sweetness of her breath with each inhalation, his mind enraptured in delight like an infant at his mother's breast, sucking her life-giving oxygen in rhythm with her pendulous tail. She was effortless motion, like the sea itself, gliding onward. His mind quickly lost all sensations; neither feeling the cold, nor the passage of time, nor the distance traveled, unaware that the induced twilight was on purpose and due to the sweet chemicals released in Shera's lungs.

The storm was to their rear but gaining on them, so she changed course to avoid the dangerous currents it generated, even while trying to keep a direct line to shore. At the end of the first day, the storm was upon them. Shera went deeper to escape the roiling water, which could easily rip Jeremy from her arms.

Swimming at a deeper depth slowed her progress and caused her to expend a greater amount of energy but what choice did she have? She only hoped for the storm to pass quickly so they could return near the surface where the water was less dense and the swimming easier. Then for further safety, they remained at the bottom almost the entire day, yet that did not stop the stirred-up currents from battering her body.

Shera searched for tides that flowed towards the shore and hoped to ride one in, reducing her effort. Luck was not on their side, the storm passed but they were still too far from shore to benefit. By the second midday, she knew she could not make it. They bobbed on the surface for the rest of the day, as she could swim no more.

Before night fell, Jeremy told her, "now, it is my turn to save you. Change to your human form." She did. Dumping the clothes from the net sack, he placed one sling over her arm and one over his, beginning to swim back out to sea, towing her along. He swam all night and long into the next day, also knowing that she was keeping him on track. If only they had been closer to shore, he could have swum until she recovered. Instead, by next nightfall, she took over again and they returned to the Sea Queen.

Both physically and mentally exhausted, they took to the Captain's bed, buried in the quilting for warmth, as both were near frozen and close to death. Wrapping his arms around her neck, Jeremy combed his fingers through her hair, then gazing into her gray green eyes he pulled her closer. Locking his lips to hers, he tasted her sweetness, this time not as an infant to his mother, but as a man to his lover.

Their bodies thawed, then warmed, and in tender motions melted together. Shera had never known the sensations that overtook her. All brought on by the touch of hands, fingers, tongue on her and his manhood in her. For all the men she had experienced in death, this was more powerful than all of them. This was joy unbounded, peace undisturbed, mania unrestricted. It was passion to the point of madness. It was love totally surrendered.

☠   ☠   ☠

Shera took Jeremy into the hull where she breathed for him, no longer afraid of their secret being uncovered, wishing in fact that they were discovered and someone would come, but she had no faith in that happening. *You might have made it to shore on your own. Why did you bring me back here?*

You would not have survived if I left you. You saved my life, I owed you no less. If we are both to survive, we need a boat, and we have one right here.

They returned to the dark of the Captain's quarters. There was so little breathable air they dared not light a lantern.

"This ship is on the bottom and has a hole in its side," Shera pointed out, "you are determined to make it your tomb."

"I have plans to raise her once more. There are enough supplies to patch the side, and with you breathing for me, I can make the repairs in a week."

"But she is still full of water."

Jeremy had considered that problem and had the perfect solution. "We will burn what is onboard. The smoke shall provide the air needed to float her to the surface."

Shera agreed. They had no other option anyway, as swimming anywhere else was out of the question.

Jeremy discovered that Shera's air had powers he did not understand, but decidedly made work easier, being able to drive nails with one swing of the hammer through a foot-thick plank. Instead of a week as he had planned, the repairs were completed in a day. He cut holes through the two main bulkheads and a small one in the hull for the water to exit through a watertight hatch. Opening the hatch, he went to find as much dry bedding, wood and ship's cargo as he could, packed it in the forecastle and used the lantern oil to start a blaze. His only concern was that the fire could weaken the decking and bring water crashing in before there was enough smoke to raise the Sea Queen.

The flame started quick and strong, smoke raced along the ceiling of the deck, and they abandoned ship through the escape hatch in the stern. The water was warmer at this depth, but he would still not last long, so the ship needed to start rising soon. They watched and waited for a sign then heard a loud crack. The bow rocked in her plot but she had been trapped by centuries of sediment. A few more creaking sounds reverberated from the old ship, then she went back to sleep once more.

Jeremy worried that the flames would burn out of control, but the true flaw in his plan was what had made it necessary in the first place, there was not enough oxygen to keep the flames alive. Now, the ship was utterly uninhabitable. *I am sorry, Shera, this is goodbye. But first, you must know that I love you. Now take me to the surface and leave me there.*

No, this is not the end. Your plan is good. You just need a better source of air.

If we had a better source of air, we would not be in dire straits. Jeremy tried to separate himself from her, but she held him fast.

There is a source of air. It is not breathable air, but we can use it to float the Sea Queen. We just need help to move the ship to the Crystal Field.

What kind of help?

It is on its way.

Within the hour, a shape appeared in the blackness. Jeremy could not tell what it was, as he had never seen anything like it, but it was huge. It rammed the stern of the Sea Queen and the ship bounced on the seabed with a thunderous boom, an ancient cloud of bones and death arising around her. When the whale swam past them, Jeremy reached out to feel its majestic power then watched as she positioned herself behind the ship again and nudged it forward.

Is this your doing, Shera?

I told you not to give up hope. Help comes to those who seek it.

They swam ahead, guiding the whale to the Crystal Field. It groaned and grunted as it pushed the heavy mass through the thick mud ten miles, the ship becoming somewhat buoyant as the air pocket inside was half the volume of the ship. Then as it entered the field of hard white sand, bubbles rose around it and the farther into the field the greater the number of bubbles effervesced from the sea floor. Released by the tremendous weight of the Sea Queen, the bubbles obscured the ship completely.

Quickly, we must open all the portals we can on one side of the ship.

They opened the gun ports, the oar ports, anything that would open on the starboard side. Shera commanded the whale to give the ship one more thump and the Sea Queen keeled over, the poisonous gas filling the ship, forcing out the water, and sending her towards the surface. They stood on deck but neither could breathe, and hoped the ship reached the surface before they choked to death.

The Sea Queen's bow broke the surface shedding water from her deck like a tremendous waterfall. Jeremy fought the onslaught of water, shells, and the debris that had built up on deck, Shera went with the flow back into the sea. When the ship returned to the daylight, she leaped onboard.

"You've done it!"

"We have done it! I would not be alive today if not for you, Shera, my love. But we can celebrate later, we need to rid the ship of its fouled air."

"Oh no!" Shera's eyes darkened.

"What is wrong?"

Without a word, Shera dove over the side and he tried to peer into the bubbling sea, seeing the water slowly returning to its calm state, now that the ship was on the surface. Now he could feel that something terrible had occurred below. Long minutes passed before she sprang from the water and landed on deck beside him, still in her natural form, lying at his feet sobbing inconsolably. Grabbing her up into his lap, he brushed the hair from her

The Emerald Lady

tortured face, knowing instantly that the whale had perished. The same gas that had floated the ship had also made it impossible for it to swim out of the Crystal Field. The great beast that had saved him from drowning had done so by drowning herself. Despair clung to them like the ice on their skin in the December air.

Chapter 5
Rehema's Curse

Jeremy lay with Shera wrapped in his embrace. In human form, she was petite in comparison to his brawny muscular size, even in his emaciated condition. Now, he was glad he had decided against burning the bed and bedding in the Captain's cabin. She pleasured him with madness born out of unbearable guilt, trying to purge her mind with this new action that drove thought and reason far from her consciousness.

Jeremy did not fully comprehend her sorrow over the death of the whale, but perhaps it had been a pet, so it might feel like the loss of a dog, which he understood. He felt somewhat ashamed at how much he enjoyed the passion she liberated in their bed. Before, both had been inexperienced, but having no idea as to what was happening to her, she reacted as nature dictated. Nowadays, she was in control of her body, even if having lost control of her mind. She poured herself into him, body and soul. She needed to.

He delighted in the soft suppleness of her breasts, the tender and thick buds he found so much joy rolling on his tongue. The power of her hips surprised him; they were small, but thrust with great vigor, feeling compelled to straddle him and perform with unrelenting motion. She was a raging storm pounding him into submission, her red locks whipped about her, with green flashes erupting between them, mesmerizing him. He released himself in her, grabbing onto her hips and digging with his nails into them until he drew blood. She expelled her spirits with equal voracious determination, clawing the skin from his chest in long and deep bloody furloughs. Their outbursts of passion echoed throughout the ship and shortly after their completion, Shera would start again. They were in a blissful twilight of love, their body heat glazing them in sweet and fragrant sweat. Exhausted and existing in the afterglow of love, the world was theirs alone.

Squeezing her tightly to him, a sudden fear took hold of Jeremy. Her world was the sea, and although he made his living from the sea, he would return to land and lose her. Because, how long could she exist in his world? He had spent two months, possibly three, underwater and was near death for it, weak and malnourished. How would she fare if forced to live a life out of the ocean? All the stories he had heard, and had not believed, had one common thread, a mermaid could not live long out of the sea. This much had to be true.

Shera shook and trembled in his arms and logically, he imagined it was from the cold. The stove in the cabin was of little use against the winter frost, as the ship had become water-logged and ice was forming all around them. A thin layer covered every inch from bow to stern, which, in his mind, although keeping it unbearably cold also kept it afloat. The extra sails had not burned, so he finally decided that in the morning he would rig the main mast and sail south to warmer waters.

But Shera's uneasy sleep had nothing to do with the temperature, she felt them approaching. The whale's death had exposed her secret and the Queen's anger was palpable. There was no sense in trying to hide anyway; no matter how much she endeavored to do so the maidens were inside her head, knowing exactly where she was and what she had done. The only time they were not in her mind was when she was out of hers. They were lost in her hours of physical pleasures, but in this tranquility, they ravished hers relentlessly.

They were coming, condemning from afar and she knew it would not be long before they reached them. She pleaded for them to take her alone, but she also discerned that the Queen wanted both to pay. She fought and tossed in her sleep and finally, Jeremy could feel the approaching hoard as well. His dreams were of storms and death, whales swallowing him and digesting him unbearably slowly. Then being thrown into an endless darkness, hearing Shera cry out in anguish, but out of sight and out of reach.

The pair of lovers awoke predawn to what sounded like wet sandbags hitting the deck above their heads. Their eyes popped open and locked, hers fiery and angry, his confused and tired. Women invaded the cabin, laying hands on Shera first and Jeremy could tell she was enraged yet offered no resistance. He, on the other hand, was determined not to be so cooperative. He lunged at them but two caught his arms in midair and another put her hands to his temples; he went limp.

Let me take him. Shera demanded.

Absolutely not. Came the response in unison.

Maidens leapt over the side with Jeremy paralyzed in their grip, a pair dragging him on his back by his outstretched arms. A third locked her mouth to his, forcing air into him. He felt her breath scorching his insides, there was nothing sweet or seductive about this mermaid. They were obviously heading somewhere and he prayed it was nearby. But no, they continued in this manner for days and nights, through the endless sea.

Then just as he believed himself beyond limit, they dove deep and out of reach of sunlight, with Shera following the lead maiden into a large cave, straight to the back and up from a pool. The pair who had transported him tossed him onto a stone slab at one end of the pool, finally letting him regain power to his limbs and muscles.

Shera looked around the darkened cavern, registering the presence of hundreds of her sisters on ledges and in pools. She glanced around again, not recognizing the place. Voices exploded in both their heads, too many for Jeremy to make sense of what was being said, but Shera heard each and every one clearly and distinctly.

The voices stopped abruptly in Jeremy's head, and all attention shifted to the woman who rose and stood over him in a red velvet dress with royal blue lace at the hem, on the sleeves, and neckline. No doubt, this was the Queen, the one Shera feared. She looked formidable but not dangerous, her skin appearing to be the texture of polished granite, smooth, with a glaze to it, and just as hard. He had imagined that she would be older but she looked about fifty; rather young to be a queen.

Foolish man, I am more than my looks belie, and more to fear than you can ever imagine. You will soon rue the day your mother set air in your lungs and light to your eyes.

"You may rule these creatures, but I hold no allegiance to you. You hold no sway over me." Jeremy told her defiantly as he stood eye to eye with her. Voices started in his head again.

Her glowing golden hair was in braids, wrapped into a crown on top of her head, her blue eyes cold and unfeeling. Lifting her hand, all was quiet once more. Each finger of her hand wore a ring carved from stones of peridot, emerald, jade, and crystals of agate, bloodstone, and citrine. She tapped his forehead and he collapsed back onto the slab.

Still think you can stand against my power? Imprudent! Shera, I commanded you to leave this man to his fate. You disobeyed and now a whale has paid for your folly.

"Is that what this is really all about? One beast has died and I feel truly sorry for that, but she saved my life," Jeremy said as he squeezed his legs, realizing that he had no feeling in them whatsoever.

See what I told you about men? There he lies, helpless as the day he came into this world and he still thinks his life is worth more than any other. All life is precious and none holds greater value in the eyes of the Creator above another.

"But it seems that some hold theirs in greater regard than that of those who serve them. I have seen your type all my life, you think your title and power gives you the right to dictate the fate of all. You can cripple me, but you cannot silence me." Jeremy's temper was rising, as was his voice and he no longer paid attention to the voices in his head. "You speak falsely of your values and beliefs. Shera came to you for help and your response was to let me die. Why? Because my form somehow offends you. I committed no crime against you, yet, you condemned me to death."

You committed no offense, that is true, but you chose your fate the moment you stepped aboard a ship. I simply commanded Shera to leave you to it. That beast you

64

speak of did not choose to aid you. It did so at Shera's command. Her actions caused its death to save you.

"She had already saved my life," Jeremy countered. "Your order was to execute me by inaction. So instead of mine, you precipitated that whale's death. I have never seen a more majestic creature and you should be ashamed that your orders caused its demise."

Clamoring erupted in the cavern but still he could not make sense of the jumble of thoughts that reverberated in his head, although, he sensed too that some had agreed with him. Others begged for leniency from the Queen and thankfully, none called for his head on a spike. But in spite of the uproar, he noticed that the one voice he would recognize anywhere had nothing to say in her own defense. It may have been more than just an old whale to her, but Shera needed to speak up for herself. He called out to her, "Shera, you know the creature's death was an accident, not your fault. You could not have known the whale would be trapped by the bubbles. Please, say something."

A chorus of support arose at that point, many in the court viewing the death as an unfortunate accident. Then they called even louder for an end to present proceedings.

But the Queen would not have her authority challenged by a man. *Yes, bring Shera before me. Let's hear how this death is nothing more than an unfortunate turn of circumstances.*

Shera climbed from the pool, transforming as she did, and passing Jeremy, touched his hand, instantly restoring the feeling to his legs. *Stay down, my love. You can do no further for me.*

Listen to her, MY LOVE, because you can only make it worse for the both of you. So, tell me, Shera, you were aware of the dangers on entering the Crystal Field, were you not? So how was this an accident, child?

This was my doing. I will accept any punishment you deem fair.

Jeremy jumped to his feet. "Whatever punishment you have in mind for her, I will take on. It was my life she saved."

"Do not imagine for one second that you will leave here without carrying the weight of your arrogance," Rehema spoke directly to him then grabbing Shera by the head, she spread her fingers wide and along the sides of her face and pressed her thumbs onto the eyelids. The stones on her hands glowed and grew hot and Jeremy heard the cavern cry out as one.

NOOOOOOO.

Since you think this man is worth the life of another, you have surrendered your fertility to him. Now, you may spend the rest of your existence in this inferior form, but never be one of them, my love. Henceforth, you must always be surrounded by the seawater which sustains you; however, you will never feel the sweetness of its froth in your lungs again.

Jeremy gasped. "You mean... that she's a mermaid who can never return to the sea? You are cruel beyond belief, but I will take care of her until the day I die, and will somehow make her life better than it could have ever been. Your curse will fade in time and she will be happy despite you."

"You will have to care for her, MY LOVE, because your life will only last as long as she is alive." Before Jeremy could defend himself, Rehema dropped Shera onto the slab and latched onto his head in the same manner, her fingers burning into the sides of his skull. He felt her power surging through his mind, creating a firestorm within. But the energy did not confine itself there; it ran down every nerve and muscle inside him, setting his skin on fire. And when Rehema released him, he too dropped like a bag of marbles.

Jeremy could feel every thought and emotion running through Shera, and it was so much more than the mental speak they had shared before. Now, he knew everything about her first-hand, her memories, her experiences, all the years of her life, all three-hundred and forty-seven. She was just a young woman, with perhaps another seven-hundred more to come. He could not comprehend that lifespan.

In contrast, Shera's mind became blank, all thoughts of her sisters erased. A great emptiness with only one other person within it, Jeremy. At once, she knew him more deeply than any other and felt the burning sensation inside his head, as if her own were ablaze. Shera was bewildered; the Queen had taken more than just her ability to transform, she had cut her out of her known world completely, and shackled her to Jeremy. She felt him body and mind. They were one.

Rehema held her hands above the two forms lying on the cold slab and forced unconsciousness upon them. Most maidens fled the cavern, only a handful remaining at Rehema's command. They gathered the two lovers and carried them away. One group headed east. The other swam west.

Chapter 6
Cast Adrift

Aberash and Raakel entered the parlor of their ancient palace in the Mediterranean town of Isamali, awaiting the Queen's daughters with some trepidation. Far removed from the Winter Waters, they were cautious nonetheless. Aberash had not been at Shera's and Jeremy's trial. First, it was not unplanned; the queen preferred cutting her out of high level court proceedings. Second, it had been held at a place where her advanced years made such a trip impractical. But she had voiced her displeasure with her sister just the same, her dissent ringing loud and clear throughout the maiden world. She, Aberash, the elected queen, had been the voice of their world for five centuries, even after Rehema took full control of the realm directly after the second split, four hundred years past. But many still held her as their true ruler.

Aberash walked out onto the balcony, looking out to sea in flowing white linen that appeared dull next to her alabaster skin and shimmering white hair. "Where are the others? Are you sure you told them the right place, Raakel?"

"Yes, sister. You do realize that you grow more impatient with each passing decade. Where else would we hold such a meeting? Rehema would not dare confront you here, or anywhere in these waters." The younger maiden was eyeing a servant with lustful intent.

"Careful, sister, he may look pleasing but some of these Egyptians have strange bed manners. Besides, you know as well as anyone that lying with one will end your maiden-bearing ability. Is that what you really want?"

Raakel stood a moment then walked around the man holding a feathered fan, her Grecian dress showing off her ample bosom and shapely long legs, "I've birthed four already, two at once in the last spawning, I won't be missing anything. Moreover, I heard talk that it is you who has developed strange bed habits in your nine-hundred years. Perhaps one of these men may be tempted to survive the experience."

"If I am too intense for these men, Raakel, I fear that you, in your youthfulness, will be much too rigorous for their frail hearts. Anyway, our sisters draw near. They will be here within the hour."

Raakel, who appeared to be in her thirties, was in fact twenty times that age. She stroked the servant's face and placed a hand over the masculine chest; his heart raced. Leaning slightly, she kissed his cheek and felt his heart rate jump higher. "Maybe you are right, sister. Outwardly, this one is a rock, but his insides I fear may be made of lesser material. Do you think it was Shera bonding with this man before she spawned at least one maiden that so outraged Rehema?"

"I cannot venture to understand the mind of our sister," Aberash returned to the parlor, waved her hand and all the men departed, leaving them alone in the marble room. Her eyes were aged but she still saw, things that many did not care about, or disregarded. One finger stroked the white linen drapes that fluttered in the gentle breeze between marble columns and her eyes fixed on the sun as it cast a purple glaze across the sky and then began a slow descent into the Mediterranean Sea. "Her mind has twisted over the centuries and become increasingly bitter to the world of men. More reclusive in our interactions with them, which perhaps is not a bad thing, but this is beyond sanity. It will do more harm than the death of one creature justifies."

Raakel's blue eyes reflected the late afternoon firmament as she joined her sister gazing westwards from the balcony, her mind focused, now that the men had been removed, "There is much dissent among the realm and I cannot see what you could possibly plan that would rectify this situation."

"Mind your thoughts, sister. You do not want to let others in before we even begin. We will wait for the others, and then find where the Queen has imprisoned the two. Perhaps, we are not too late."

"Too late for what?"

"To avoid war," Aberash's gray eyes radiated with the memories of the past.

Shreya and Shahira arrived at the palace through an underwater passage that led directly to the throne room. Gowns and robes awaited them. They dressed quickly and made their way to the top floor parlor to meet their aunts. Wine, fruit, and nuts lay around the room on ornate tables. The newcomers were famished and ate wildly, having swum nonstop across the Atlantic Ocean. In the parlor, they were as far from their sea life as they could be.

"We have heard nothing of our sister in a week," Shreya said as she took a deep breath. "The Queen has blocked our minds from her. Even our natural bonds are being hindered."

"No, it is not you who is being blocked from her," Aberash explained, "she has altered her physical being, changed her at the core of her very existence, created an abomination; neither maiden nor woman is she now. She merely exists outside of our world, and theirs."

"There are many, hundreds, who feel the Queen has gone too far," Shahira announced. "But with you, Aberash, at the front again, she will have to resign as Queen. You can then remove the curse."

"She will never step down peacefully," Aberash disagreed. "She has many supporters, and many more who will not oppose her over the life of a man."

"But..."

"Shahira, I did not summon you here to speak of confrontation," she rebuked the young maiden. "Furthermore, even if Rehema agreed to abdicate, only she can reverse the curse. Some may follow me to war, but they will not afterwards. I am too old to take the scepter back, and we cannot open our world to war."

"Then why did you summon us?" questioned Shreya.

"The three of you must travel to Emfopotno and seek Ehecatl..."

"What? No!" Raakel yelled. "You are as mad as the Queen. You want us to go seek out a dragon? He hates man, and is not particularly fond of us either. Ehecatl will more than likely eat the three of us, before he ever hears the first word of our plight."

"I agree with Raakel, aunt. What possible aid could a dragon give us, and why do you believe that he would?" Asked Shreya.

"For one thing, he is the only one who can locate Shera and Jeremy," explained the matriarch. "And another, he is the last of his kind. All his children have paid dearly for his transgressions; he must now make amends for the state of the world. After all these millennia, I think he is ready to do that."

The three maidens voiced their opposition and tried to dissuade her but Aberash's mind was clearly made up.

She gave them a singular gift for the dragon and told them that it should keep them safe. The three younger maidens exchanged quizzical glances between themselves, then, aware that nothing would change Aberash's mind, they returned to eating and drinking, for who knew when they would do so again so lavishly and undoubtedly needed all their strength for the journey to Emfopotno.

Soon after, Raakel called for the servant she had been eyeing earlier, taking him to her chambers, also telling her sister, "If I am to become a meal for a dragon, at least this man might mourn my passing."

"If I am wrong about this, I will mourn your death."

"I am sure that you will," Raakel jested, "but I would rather that he does. And if I am not eaten, then I also have something to come back to."

The three traveled from Isamali to the Red Sea, where they began their swim to the Indian Ocean, towards Eastern India; a short trip, considering the journey to Emfopotno. Short, but vastly dangerous, especially as they would be traversing tiger shark domain. All sharks were

James L Hill

dangerous to maidens, but tiger sharks the worst. Being loners, solitary predators were harder to control, and listened to no one.

But three watching out for each other should be safe enough, even if having to limit their mental communications. Which was in fact a necessity in order to keep their mission secret, because if the Queen got scent of where they were headed, she would dispatch others to stop them. Once they reached land, they would be almost undetectable but until then, limited interactions also meant greater vulnerability to shark attacks.

They swam in pyramid formation, Shahira out front as she was the youngest and had the keenest crystal blue eyes, her black skin and hair making her less of a target. She was able to swim right up to the beasts and give them a thump to scare them off. Additionally, she was long and powerfully built, presenting a daunting figure that none but the oldest of sharks would attack. Shreya and Raakel completed the base, swimming parallel to each other several yards apart and several more behind Shahira, swishing their tails in harmony, to give the appearance of being a much larger creature.

The camouflage worked well, leaving them unimpeded across the Indian Ocean, until they got closer to shore. There, a large tiger shark with an appetite to match its fifteen-foot size, locked onto the dark figure with brilliant blue eyes and charged. Shahira spun at the moment of impact and swatted sharply against its gills with her tail. The other two followed suit, whacking it

75

again on either side as they passed, the stinging rebuke discouraging the beast from pursuing them further.

They arrived at the Shahbazpur Channel near sunset. Soon, it would be hard to detect the fishermen and their nets, so they decided to push on, heading up the river to Pankhabari. They reached the small fishing village before sunrise, and exited the water under the light of a full moon.

Raakel and Shreya wore simple saris while Shahira took on the appearance of an Indian Prince. Her male disguise would make it easier to blend among the local population, move in the markets and to acquire transportation up the Himalayas without using their mental powers. She was also more comfortable in male garb and body, as her six-foot-two figure carried rippling chest muscles as opposed to the suppleness of her breast in maiden form. She pulled her coal black hair into a ponytail, which was rather short for a maiden, but let it hang down to the middle of her back from underneath the red and gold turban. Her golden sherwani had seven ruby buttons down the front and the silk pajamas were royal blue with matching gold trim at the cuff. At four-hundred and twelve, her features were still soft, which added to her look of a convincing Nizam. She also wore a gem-encrusted scabbard that held a bejeweled handle sword.

"You make a very desirable man, my sister," Raakel commented.

The other two studied her oddly. Aberash had warned them of her coupling with the servant and that she might become erratic.

Shahira began bartering with a local trader who had a team of horses and mules. It was late in the year to travel past the foothills, so he kept pointing out that it was particularly dangerous to go where she wanted him to take them. She offered triple the worth of his whole team of a horse, two mules, and a cart to take them to the Temple of the Dragon, while withholding their true destination, which was further up the mountain and only reachable by climbing.

"No one has been there in hundreds of years," argued the man, "why would you want to take such a dangerous trip?"

"We have angered the gods and need to make amends," said Shahira, sure that he would not stand in the way of a holy pilgrimage. After all, he could risk incurring the gods' wrath upon himself and his family by denying them the help they sought.

"I will take your wife, all the way to Emfopotno myself, you and your second wife can wait here for our return."

Raakel, what are you doing? Is this some kind of joke you are playing? Even on land it is dangerous to use our powers in this manner.

I play no tricks now. We travelled three days to reach this far, the journey to Emfopotno and back will be ten time longer. It is a full moon now, but if we do not make it back to the sea before the next we will be trapped in the land of men forever. I am sure Aberash failed to mention that fact.

Shreya confessed then. *I know the distance to the dragon's lair and it is true that the trip will be even more perilous on land. But one will not survive alone, which is why she sent us together. We must make it there, and fate will decide if we make it back in time, or suffer the same consequences as our sister, Shera.*

Did no one trust to confide these facts to me? Shahira demanded from her sisters.

Would you have declined to come along had you known? Queried Shreya.

No, of course not.

Then there was no need to burden you with that detail. It would become evident in time.

"My Prince, I will take you and your wives to the temple and wait there. Perhaps, the gods will show favor on me as well."

"Of course they will," Shahira assured the old man. "They have already brought you a year's wages in one day. Now, we need to leave right away."

The guide started by first helping the two women into the cart with the supplies and Shahira onto the horse's back, then he handed the prince a musket and pistol. "They are primed and ready. You will want to be keeping the power dry."

"What are these for? We will have no need for weapons where we are going," Shahira assured him. Guns would serve no purpose if the dragon had no wish to aid them.

78

"Maybe not where you are going," he agreed, "but you may need them to get there. This time of year, tigers are hungry and fierce."

"I cannot kill another creature."

"You will probably not hit it anyway," he laughed at the shocked expression on the young man's face. "The sound will be enough to scare them away. But do try."

They traveled for days going northeast along a trade route, the road winding through the jungle, narrowing in places barely wide enough to get the cart across, night and day unknown sounds besieging their ears. A week into that leg of the journey and they were further from the sea than they had ever been, perhaps further than any maiden had ever been, yet they were less than halfway to the base of the mountains.

Snow-covered mountaintops beckoned them onward, the hard road tortured their bodies, and secretly, each wished for a soothing pool to transform in and stretch out the sore muscles. But there were only small shallow swiftly running streams and no solitude to reveal their true form.

After ten days on the road, they saw their first tiger. It was lying in the brush eyeing the convoy with great interest. Shahira eyed the beast back, commanding it to be still. She was not sure if it listened and obeyed, as she had no real experience with land creatures but it did not attack.

They broke through the jungle the next day and began an even more arduous trek up the mountain trail to the Temple of the Dragon. It took another three to reach the plateau.

The temple was carved into the granite mountain, old, pre-dating the three maidens with ease. It was immense, stretching for miles in both directions, and cavernous, tunnels and chambers snaking deep into the earth. Some bore the marks of hammer and chisel. Others, much more ancient, had smooth walls of melted rock, with carvings and drawings throughout. Several depicted great battles and Raakel was quick to recognize scenes from the two Great Splits. Near the entrance, armies of men in their thousands did battle with the dragons of the skies. Machines of war and flaming clouds told the story of the Second Great Split between Mankind and Molytan. Deeper in the mountain, the First Great Split between Maiden and Molytan was depicted as huge floods and fiery mountains. Pictures rife with winged beasts being pulled down into the sea or fish bodies boiling in lakes of fire. Raakel became deeply saddened in those tunnels.

Water poured from several openings in the rock, calling to the maidens, tempting them to change to their natural selves and stay in the many pools inside the chambers. But this was fresh water from rain and melting snow, it could offer a little comfort but not save their lives or stop them from losing their powers. After a day's rest,

Raakel released their guide. *Go home, and may the gods smile upon your family today.*

They followed a path through the sanctuary, which led them out of a crevice, miles above the temple. From there, they would have to climb the face of the mountain. The rocks were sharp and cold as was the wind and the thin atmosphere made breathing difficult. By the end of the day, they had scaled the mountain further than any man ever had, and were several days from the top.

Shreya began feeling the eyes of the dragon on them, soon after the others felt it too, and all knew that Ehecatl was not pleased they were coming.

They climbed without stopping for rest or sleep another week and finally reached the summit as a blizzard descended and whipped them from all sides, their flimsy clothing no use in the harsh environment. Caked in snow and ice they approached Ehecatl's den with difficulty, all thinking that death might taste better. But the roar of the wind was no match for the flaming breath of the mighty wind dragon, the yellow flames blinding them as if they had suddenly been exposed to the sun, the heat immediately clearing and drying the ground, warmed their bodies and saved them from freezing to death mere feet from the spot where they knew they had reached their limit.

Speak sea-witches! What can be so important that you risk the very essence of your existence to journey to my dwelling?

Do not pretend you do not know what has transpired in the world below. Your eyes are everywhere, Ehecatl. And although you have retreated to the roof of the world, you are still concerned with the turns fate has taken. Raakel peered into the dark hole in the ground from where the dragon had exhaled his great heat.

He warmed the air on top of the mountain so much that it pushed back the blizzard and they were now standing in bright sunshine in the eye of the storm. Two glowing bright red orbs appeared in the darkness, Raakel hoped it was his eyes and not his nostrils flaring up for another blast.

Ehecatl's long black snout emerged from the darkness, the first time in centuries. It was wide, thick, and leathery. His nostrils a pair of caverns wide enough to inhale all three into their fiery pits and Shahira and Shreya grabbed Raakel's hands and tried not to let their terror show. All were doing a bad job of it.

Aberash sent you all this way to speak to me. Let me hear what she has to say.

Come forth oh Great Spirit of the Wind and hear what I have to tell you. Aberash sat on her throne at the bottom of her pool, watching the scene through her sisters' eyes. It strengthened them knowing that she was with them.

Ehecatl's head appeared above ground, his front claws shaking the mountaintop as he planted them on either side of the maidens. Effortlessly, he slid his massive body into view, spread and stretched his wings, blocking out the sky above the trio. Towering above them, he pointed his head straight up and exhaled a massive plume of fire, blowing away the remnants of the storm that had begun closing in again, the rustle of his tail creating a roaring wind, sending an avalanche of snow down the mountainside. He settled on all fours and crouched down to be eye level with the three emissaries. *You have my full attention, Mistress Sea-witch.*

I need you to locate the two lovers, as none can hide from your sight.

Why would I help either of you? Mermaids turned against my kind, Man hunted us, driving us into the heights and the cold. Now, you will turn on each other. This thing your Queen has done... She thinks it will punish them, but she has in fact put in motion the means for your kind's end. Man hunts until there is no more, it is their nature.

And all that has happened to you and your kind is of your own doing. You, Ehecatl, caused the split. Are you not ready to see it mended?

The dragon rolled his back, each spike rising and dropping; then, he inhaled deeply, almost sucking them in. His mind went dark to them, and they found themselves plastered against his mouth. It was hot and hard like burning coal. They prepared for the worst.

You have something, don't you? What have you got to trade for my assistance?

Show him.

The maidens took a few steps back; Raakel grabbed the bag from her shoulder, and pulled out an intricately carved stone globe with jade and ruby insets. She held it up to his eye. *This is a map of the remaining nesting places of your kin. You can revive your lineage if you help us. Ehecatl, once and for all rectify the erroneous deeds of all our pasts.*

The dragon's eyes grew as bright as the sun then exhaling hard, he almost blew the trio off the mountaintop. *What is to stop me from reducing these three to ash and taking your globe now?*

The fact that it will be of no use to you without me to decipher the markings. Aberash stood in her pool and looked up to the sky. *And if you think you can get to me, fire demon, I will send men to destroy every nest and then dive to the darkest part of the ocean. Do we understand each other?*

So, you merely need me to find your two lovers and you will give me the globe and its secrets?

That, and return my maidens to the sea. They have less than three days before the full moon is upon them, no time to ever make it down on their own.

Rising onto his hind legs, Ehecatl flapped his wings, stirring up a hurricane that swept the trio up into the sky. Clouds gathered, encasing the maidens, and as the globe was ripped from Raakel's hands, Ehecatl caught it with his right claw. *I know not where Queen Rehema has taken the maiden. She hides her from all light. But I send your three agents to the man's aid now. They will be there before the sun changes houses.* And flapping his wings once more, he pushed the cloud off the mountain.

All the maidens could hear was the constant roll of thunder and all they could feel was the rushing wind at their back as they sailed along in a ship of pure white water. They were disoriented, possessing no sense of position, direction, or speed; time unknown in this vessel of wind and water vapor. Then all of a sudden, they rained down into the sea, mere feet from the Sea Queen.

Rehema reached out to two of her sisters, Abene the oldest living maiden, and her youngest, Raanan. *I need you two in my throne room. There has been a development which threatens to undo us all.*

I know it too. We must join together to stop Aberash before she destroys what our mothers' mothers' mothers gained for us. Responded Abene then joined the Queen with an escort of five hundred maidens, spawns of her spawns, all loyal to their matriarchal lineage, filling the great chamber of the throne room inside Usea Maya.

Raanan came with her two daughters, who were barely out of their childhood; and sat wide-eyed stroking the Queen's fins in an attempt to calm her down. But Rehema was not to be pacified and swatted her sister from the pool, sending her crashing onto the hard stone cavern floor. Her two daughters swam through the hole behind the throne and came out of the pool nearest their mother, helped her back into the water, and stroked her forehead and temple with seawater to ease the pain.

Sorry, Raanan, but see what your niece has done to me? They plot against us and side with our enemy. We must put a stop to this... this treachery, before it is too late.

Ah, but it is already too late, sister Queen.

Aberash! Do you want my throne that badly that you will set free what took millennia to lock away? Apollonia gave the scepter to me and with it the job of keeping all maidens safe, including you, dear sister. We will thwart your attempt at unleashing the dragons.

Apollonia handed you the power because I was still lost in my own tragedies, and at the time I thought you would make a good Queen. And you were. But your heart has changed, sister. Your daughter is full of mercy as you once were, but now you only seek revenge for past wrongs.

The maidens started thrashing furiously in the pool waters, the din growing as thunder. Then, it rang out from the mouth of the cavern, raising a dense fog within the walls of the throne room. So thick was the vapor, they could see Aberash's face in the mist. The cloud rose higher, broke through the cavern's mouth, and spread out as a dark storm over the sea. As dark as the Queen's thoughts, and aimed directly at Aberash. Elements ripped the skies, ominous clouds billowing across the Mediterranean, and men turned their boats to shore attempting to escape the building squalor. Thunder rolled and shook the palace walls and lightning struck the marble facades in Isamali.

Aberash sat on her throne on the edge of the pool, studying the swirling waters with interest. The vision was that of the Sea Queen entangled in a massive bed of seaweed in the Windless Sea, the ship baking under the Equatorial sun. Its hull, decks, and masts becoming brittle and fragile in the unrelenting heat. Jeremy was red and burnt, excruciating pain racking him to his soul, thinking of nothing else outside of burning flesh. And ever-present under the layer of agony, Shera.

The waters of Aberash's pool became cloudy and dark. *You want to know how the man fares, sister. Enter the waters and see for yourself.*

You can blind me, Queen, but you cannot stop what I have put in motion. I make this single plea now; undo what has been done to these two. Return them to what they were and let us find another way to deal with this situation. Together we can right the past wrongs.

Very well, it seems that you have decided to bring about the Third Great Split. So be it! You, Man, and the Molytan shall suffer this day forevermore.

Chapter 7
The Great War

Aberash felt the swell of heartache rise like the tide and she instantly crossed the expanse of time, falling back through the centuries as effortlessly as an autumn leaf from a tree. Old wounds opened and began to bleed as freshly as the day they had first been inflicted. The waters of her pool ran crimson and her body shivered with the onrush of memories she would rather not relive.

No matter how painful those days had been, especially those marking the end of the Second Split to live through, they became worse every time she recalled them. It had caused such a schism in her heart that she had not spawned another maiden since. For centuries, she carried the weight of loss in her soul, mired in self-recrimination, pity and unforgiveness. She could be no queen.

The war between Maiden and Dragon decimated their numbers radically. Their mothers had fought persistently and valiantly for an eternity but ultimately had to turn to Mankind for aid. Men's numbers grew fast after the First Split, procreating rapidly and yearly, after the first decade. They might have lost longevity of life but gained its abundance, and numbers was the only thing that could defeat Ehecatl and his hoard.

Ehecatl proclaimed himself the Dragon King and ruler of all Molytans and gave them a new direction. No longer were they to be the undertakers of the weak and dying, despising the task of cleaning up the world. He would initiate the death of those who were weaker or opposed him. He had become death.

A breath of fire converted Molytans from their energetic corporeal state to Dragons and those who refused transformation were summarily eaten. Ehecatl, sensing rising rebellion in some, prevented them from being transformed, wanting none to challenge his authority and in desperation, the remaining Molytans reached out to Maidens. And thus, began the First Great War.

Dragons could not get to maidens who remained in the oceans, as bottomless waters made them immune to fire and dragons could not dive deep enough to eat them, but in order to fight, maidens had to surface. It was then they were wholly vulnerable and easily overpowered, as few things could harm dragons. Iron could hold one for a time, but that was provided a maiden could shackle it. Black metal could not pierce their thick hide, so the more dragons killed and consumed, the bigger and denser they became.

However, maidens had one weapon that never failed. Dragons, like all creatures, were susceptible to mind-speak. A concerted effort by maidens, especially of the same family line, was the most effective at subduing the beasts long enough to chain them. Or, as it became increasingly necessary, to get them to follow maidens deep underwater until they drowned. Aided by an army of men and her two daughters, Angelica and Aja, Aberash set out to capture one of the most formidable dragons terrorizing the African continent.

Unaizah had set himself up in the desert as far from water as he could possibly be; knowing that maiden powers weakened as they travelled inland. The hot dry sands and blast furnace of winds would make their ability to lead men against him futile. Coupled with his own army of men, who served him out of fear, gave him reign over the desert kingdom for a thousand years. Unsurprisingly, his was one of the last dragon kingdoms to remain unchallenged. The fall of the northern kingdom after the Battle of Hastings saw Man and Maiden forming alliances against all Dragons around the world, so some fixed their attention on defeating Unaizah.

Moreover, he was supreme in his land and had defeated all that marched against him, whipping up sandstorms at will, and burning armies a hundred strong with a single breath. Unaizah ordered his people, Molytan and men alike, to construct a castle of sandstone that towered above the dunes. White spires were visible from all sides across the desert, day and night, the three largest towers appearing as one in constant flux.

He delighted in flying out from the towers during the day to blacken tiny sandstone hovels below, feeding on the fear his shadow caused as well as the sacrifices he demanded and citizens paid. For if his yearly fill of flesh was not delivered to the castle promptly, he burnt villages and their inhabitants to ash. None were allowed to leave his domain, and once within sight of the towers, they were trapped. Anyone trying to venture beyond his sight would soon hear the roar of wind from his wings and feel the blast of hellfire from his mouth.

Aberash was in her fourth century when she was approached by a Molytan named Heine. He had escaped the African desert during a sandstorm and travelled to the Mediterranean Sea seeking a maiden and found Aberash and her two young daughters. Heine was old, in fact, ancient, going back to the time before Ehecatl's changing and he gave her the knowledge on how to kill a dragon on land.

She had known of Unaizah, as several other maidens had already tried and failed to put an end to his reign. Maidens knew of only one way to extinguish a dragon's fire and that was by drowning but in Unaizah's case, it was not an option. Heine told her that a dragon's fire was not eternal, that dragons needed sunlight to maintain their power.

"Well, there be no shortage of that in a desert," Aberash retorted as she studied Heine. Recalling stories of Molytans who had been used as bait for maidens, purporting that they had come to help rid an area of their dragon overlord but instead had led them into merciless ambushes and certain death.

"He has become old and slow-minded from centuries of being overfed," explained Heine. "With your mental powers you can lead him into a trap."

"Are you sure it is not I who is being led to the slaughter? As you know perfectly well my powers will be diminished."

Heine was not surprised by Aberash's response; there was much mistrust between the two races. He calmly explained his strategy and let her decide if she was willing to join him in his mission.

Angelica travelled ahead of her mother and sister up the Nile to the great lake known as The Lake of Fire. She was a little over two-hundred and her mental powers were strong enough to lead men; they followed and obeyed her, although she barely looked like an adult. She commanded an army of ten thousand that camped on the eastern edge of the desert, standing before them tall and slender, looking like an angel in her shining armor. Their presence did not go unnoticed to Unaizah.

Aberash and Aja travelled through the Red Sea and joined an army of African warriors approaching from the south. Aja had to stay close to her mother because at just one hundred years old her powers were weak and unreliable. Aberash would rather go to battle with her mother and sisters but they were busy at other locations, thus, as she oversaw this part of the world, Unaizah was her problem. Besides, Heine's plan was simple and should work even with maidens as young as her daughters.

His idea did not call for maidens to confront the despot dragon directly in the desert. Knowing that Unaizah would send his army out, the maidens would convert them first. But in order to get him to send his army, Aberash sent her forces towards the castle. As they engaged the dragon's men, fifty thousand Nubian spearmen, Aberash and Aja continued north to join with Angelica.

It appeared as if his forces were turning away the interlopers until Unaizah realized who was behind the attack. He could now feel the daughter of Apollonia twisting his troops to her will, drawing them away, taking them to the highlands, where others awaited with iron manacles. Aberash's mother had chained and drowned more dragons than any other maiden, he refused to fall victim to her daughter so easily. Taking to the sky, he flew straight up.

His wings ached from the lack of use; clearly, he had been idle in the castle for too long. Molytans and Nubians had gorged him with slaves to keep him appeased, now they revolted, imagining him too weak to fight; a blunder they would pay heavily for. He circled high above the castle, soaking up the sun's energy, stretching and flexing his muscles for all to see. Then he dove over the first village he came to and with a single roar burnt it to ashes. Searing breath exploded bricks out of walls, pools and wells dried up, people evaporated in the blur of flames, and nothing was left to denote that a town had ever existed.

Unaizah flapped his wings and rose once more to become a black cloud of death, circling and searching for the next target. Swelling with power until his heart shone white through his black leathery chest, he dove again and unleashed a torrent of white hot gas on the fleeing populace below. It made no difference if they were running for safety or huddled inside their homes for shelter, the town and its residents ceased to be in an instant.

Unaizah repeated the pattern over and over as he worked his way northeast towards the maidens and their armies, and with each town he destroyed, he felt more powerful, more alive, and ecstatic. He had not felt this good in a hundred years; no, two hundred, and he had Aberash to thank for it. *I will do you a kindness for returning me to my former self. I will not burn you, I shall consume you whole. Your life shall become my life. And that of your daughters too!*

Aberash joined Angelica on the shores of the great lake. The men had erected towering iron shields and positioned themselves behind them. Three levels of archers were on the ledges behind the barricades and would try to strike the only spot on the dragon where they could inflict pain, his eyes. And behind them, massive iron nets attached to boulders on catapults ready to fire, hid buried in the sandy soil. Aberash hoped the dragon would make good on his threat and went to ground.

If Unaizah remained in the air, capture was all but impossible, and he undoubtedly knew this, but he was still a dragon and could be goaded into fighting a battle on her terms. Before the first arrow could fly, Unaizah landed with an earth-quaking boom but too far out of reach for any of their weapons to be effective.

So, old and tired are you, would you like us to come closer? I don't believe you can eat anyone from there.

Unaizah erected himself on his hind legs and flapped his wings, hurling a storm of rocks and sand towards them. Their barricade held but the black metal nets lay exposed around them.

I am feeling fine, just wanted to see what I am up against. But I see that you have not changed your tactics in all these years. Like your mothers before you, you think you will drown me.

Leaping into the air, he flew high over their heads, passed them by and circled the lake behind them. Then charging at them, he blew fire across the surface of the water, raising a thick steam cloud over the lake as it roiled from the heat. Unaizah soared pass them and turned back but this time, he started his fire attack at their front line and continued until he ran out of breath over the middle of the lake, turning it into a boiling cauldron; dead fish popped up and floated on the surface.

Unaizah landed near where he had before and began walking towards them with deliberate and carefully placed steps, absorbing the picture before him of men dying in the hundreds. *Oh, how I will feast this day. Roasted men, and maiden soup. If you thought of dragging me to the bottom of the lake... We shall see who lasts longer.*

Run daughters! Take shelter in the caves.

Unaizah charged as the maidens scrambled to the rocky outcrop in the sand. On land, he was slow, his big belly dragging on the ground, and running, as slow as it was, shortened his breath and consequently the power of his flame. The maidens took shelter behind the huge iron shields as they made their way to the opening of the caves. Unaizah was further impeded in his attempt to eat Aberash and her daughters by the net that was suddenly hurled at him, as it wrapped around his snout and head. He raised himself on his hind legs, planning to use his front claws to rip the iron links apart.

So intent was he on devouring the three, he drew too close to the line of shields and a few Nubian spears landed in his left eye. The dragon howled in pain, a sound none had heard before, lashed out with his tail, and sent men and iron into the boiling water. Shaking his head violently, he tossed spears and bloody eye from its socket.

I can still see you with one good eye. And smell your fishiness. You can't hide from me in those caves.

The small rocky hills sunk deep into the sand. It was honeycombed with caves, some large and spacious, others narrow and cramped. All leading down and away from sunlight.

We split up. Stay in the small passages.

Unaizah found a large opening and quickly went in but within minutes found himself in total darkness. The scent of the three maidens was everywhere and he could hear their thoughts bouncing inside his head, taunting him. In anger, he slammed his head against the walls and clawed huge gashes out then blew clouds of fire in the hope of finding his prey in the momentary glow.

Aberash continued goading him. *Ah dragon, you are not so fearsome when you cannot flap your wings.*

Unaizah roared and his tail smashed a wall.

Aberash laughed, as she and her daughters kept working their way through tunnels that led to the lake. But they could not leave too soon. Heine's plan was to use the iron shields to seal off the entrance and trap the dragon in the dark where he would shrivel up and die.

Angelica was the first to reach a passage that led into the lake and called out. *Mother, the water still boils! We are trapped!*

Fear not children, we must stay hidden until the dragon sleeps. Then we will walk right past him and out. I feel he weakens already.

Disoriented, Unaizah trashed around in the darkness for hours then frustrated, he clawed and dug, causing walls to crumble, turning small channels into large caverns and destroying passageways back to the surface. Days of bitter blackness followed. Outside, the army of men wasted no time putting the iron shields in place. His earth-quaking movements bringing boulders down around the metal, finally sealing the caves from the outside. Certain they had seen the last of the dragon, they dispersed.

Unaizah realized the maidens had tricked him when he felt himself growing weak and tired. As a last resort, he blew fire one last time and drove up the temperature under the rocks.

Aja panicked and ran, right into the dragon's open mouth.

He bit down quickly; slicing her body into a dozen pieces then gulped her down.

Aberash and Angelica felt the loss just as if they had been stabbed by a dozen daggers. Horrified, they wished there was something they could do to hasten the monster's death. But there was not.

Angelica was trying to make her way to her mother when three giant nails from the dragon's claw burst through the earth. She eluded his grasp and hurried back the way she had come, and there she stayed, stiff with fear against a wall.

A day later, the dragon used its tail to pound her into a bloody mass. Each thrust of his tail pushing into the tight opening smashing her against the wall she had clung to for safety. Each jab breaking bone and sending unbearable pain searing through her once perfect body. So much agony she could not find the strength to even cry out, then, he inhaled her into his mouth.

Unaizah's body shrank in the eternal night, going from a sixty-foot long behemoth weighting tons to a childlike lizard no larger than a household pet in just a few days. He quietly lay down and stopped breathing. His body decayed into ooze until all that was left was a small crystalline heart.

Aberash left the caves through a watery opening a week later, but she never left the darkness. The anguish of her daughters' final moments replaying continually in her mind, reliving every sharp swipe, painful blow, and deadly bite. Every maiden felt them too but also learnt something important from the experience; they now had a way of destroying the dragons. They needed to drive the monsters from the light and they in turn would wane and die.

Ehecatl also took something from the battle, the knowledge that the Molytan Heine had betrayed them. For not only had Heine enlightened their adversaries about a dragon's need for sunlight but he had also armed the

Nubians with a new weapon. The spear-heads which had taken Unaizah's eye had been crafted from the white fire crystal, the hardest stone unearthed, and with enough force it could pierce the skin of any dragon. This combined information, gave Maiden and Mankind the power to destroy dragons.

He ordered all remaining Molytans to be transformed. He would swell their ranks, attack Man and Maiden alike, and put an end to the maidens. Without them to strengthen and block fear from men's minds, men would fall easily before the might of the dragons. He ordered his legions to take to the mountains and draw Maiden from their life-sustaining seas any way they saw fit.

Ehecatl searched for the traitor Heine himself, knowing that he had left the Nubian desert as soon as Unaizah had become entombed.

Heine was no fool, in fact, smarter than many gave him credit, he was very much aware that the maidens would either escape through the lake or die within the rocks, which he hoped would not happen. If by luck or ingenuity the trio made it out alive then his part in the death of Unaizah would become known to Mankind, Maiden, Molytan and most importantly, to their reviled dragon masters. Over the centuries, Mankind had lost their mental powers, their time becoming so short and their lives so full that they no longer took time to listen, calling it all myth. But the others did.

The maidens heard it in the ceaseless waves of the oceans, the Molytans and Dragons heard about the deeds performed that day in the rustling of trees and in the whipping winds.

Heine went south, into the deepest and thickest jungle in Africa, his light dim with age, his translucent skin opaque and browning. Soon, he would absorb no more energy from the sun and his days would be over, that was what he wanted. What he did not want was for one of the dragons to locate him, breathe their perverted fire upon him and convert him into one of them, an ageless killer. Existing merely to consume flesh and destroy life.

This had been his reason for betraying the Molytan secret to Aberash, the Maiden Queen to be, for none other was strong enough to stand against the will of Ehecatl. To be eaten or turned was the same fate to the Molytan, either way, they would be no more. Not a single Molytan had reached this late stage of life; how he looked forward to letting his fire go out peacefully. So, in a simple grass burrow, he let a single ray of light nourish him daily. For six minutes at noon, the sun shone in through the roof. His heart raced less each day and he inhaled slighter when it did. Peace would soon be his.

But Ehecatl arrived at noon on Heine's last day. Instead of a final ray of sunlight to send him into oblivion, it was dragon fire that lit up the hovel, also setting alight the jungle for a mile around. Heine felt an energy he had never known existed; he was stronger, more powerful than he had ever been. His body twisted, turned, stretched and steel-like skein of muscle unwound beneath his blackened skin, and he yearned to fly again. No, he needed to take flight as if an invisible harness was tied to his heart and held by the sun. And he hungered.

I wanted you to know what you were giving up. What you would never be able to enjoy. I wanted you to know, if only for the briefest of moments, what true power feels like.

Ehecatl stood on Heine's chest, his claws digging deep, his hind legs pinning him to the smoldering earth, the weight driving him into the crystalized ground. Ehecatl's wings blocked out the power of the sun then he opened his mouth as wide as he could. Heine stared at the fifty-foot-long daggers that were Ehecatl's triple row of teeth above him, all dripping hatred. He closed his eyes and felt two plunge into his chest. Ehecatl bit right through him and into the earth below, hearing a crackling and crunching sound as he tore out Heine's heart, breaking three teeth crushing the chrysalis in his mouth before swallowing it.

Heine's body turned to jelly then to black slime as it slipped between the claws of the dragon. He was the last of the Molytan and his betrayal had cost them all their lives in one way or another, but none with such vengeance as his own had ended. From that day forth, Dragons considered themselves immortal. Ehecatl, King of the Wind and ruler of all life, ordered the skies to be darkened by dragon wings and the earth set ablaze with fire. From east to west, north to south, every dragon obeyed. They rained destruction down on all, before taking to the tops of the world.

Chapter 8
Origins

The three maidens plunged into the thick green tangle of seaweed as tall as trees and instantly transformed to their natural state. They were sore and weak from the journey and would have liked nothing more than to sink to the bottom and sleep for a decade. But quicker than the seawater could infuse their bodies with life-giving nourishment, their minds were bombarded by dark thoughts. This form of mental communication was foreign to Shreya and Shahira and it felt as painful as a knife through the heart. Raakel had never experienced it either, but she had long known it was possible. On occasion, it had been used to drive men mad, causing them to steer ships unto rocks, but it had never been used against another maiden, until now.

Raakel thrashed through the dense growth of weeds to gather the two younger maidens to herself. She placed her fingers to their temples in the Knowing and they did likewise to her and each other, the weeds cocooning them as they reached out to Aberash for strength and healing. Voices hushed, images faded, and the quietude of the sea took over, lulling them into a much-needed remedial slumber.

Moonlight called them from their sleep. The seaweed was so thick it was easier to transform and walk through the underwater forest than to swim the few feet to the ship. They climbed aboard and immediately noticed Jeremy lying on deck, his body blistered from end to end. The Queen had him trussed fully naked and exposed.

Shahira leaned over him - his breathing was unperceivable - and stretched out a hand to reach for his forehead.

Do not touch him, sister. Even the breeze from a gull's wing will be agonizing. Informed Raakel. *Go get crystals of moonstone, rose quartz, agate, hematite, and aquamarine to begin. Shreya, start weaving a shelter from the seaweed, he needs to be covered before the sun rises again.*

Raakel stood over Jeremy and let a single teardrop fall from her blue eye. It struck his forehead and sizzled as it was instantly absorbed into the skin. A shiver raced through his body and if he had had air left in his lungs his scream would have shattered the glass of the night sky.

She let a second tear fall, landing it next to the first. It might as well have been a musket shot for all the pain he felt. And so she stood throughout the night, letting her tears nourish his ravished body one drop at a time, like a mother nursing her newborn, doing for him as she had for her daughters, when they were fresh from her womb. She herself was not yet fully recovered from their ordeal on the mountain, but she had to do what she could to quicken his recovery. It was clear the Queen had not just cursed the lovers; she meant to torment and torture them indefinitely.

They cast the seaweed nets over the lowest yardarms and created a tent which covered the entire deck, not letting a single ray of sunlight fall upon it. They set the crystals on the gunnels around the ship to cast their protection and healing power onto Jeremy and the Sea Queen as well.

Other maidens began arriving in the most desolate of places, and without a word, they set to work, clearing the seaweed jungle around the ship, and wove tents to replenish the ones that burnt up each day.

The Windless Sea was nothing more than a graveyard for ships and sailors alike, for any that was blown or drifted into those waters became helplessly trapped. Without wind to fill sails and seaweed as solid and strong as trees to resist any oarsman's might, ships languished in the cloudless sunshine day after day. The seaweed would eventually crush the hull and pull the vessel down in pieces. Sailors ran out of water and burnt to death underneath a blazing golden sun, and any who thought of swimming for his life would sooner give it up to the ensnaring seaweed leaves. Rehema had had the Sea Queen towed there, never to leave again. Neither her, nor Jeremy.

On the third fullness of the moon, they lifted Jeremy off the deck carefully and carried him into the water, as the life-giving power of the sea was amplified on that particular night, Shreya breathing for him as dozens of maidens surrounded them and lay hands on him. A month in the sun had cooked every thought from his mind, except one, Shera. Then, they returned him to the Captain's cabin where they continued to nurse him daily.

Twenty-four maidens were now onboard acting as the crew of the Sea Queen. By day, they bathed Jeremy in crystal filtered light, and by night they took him into the sea when the moon was at its highest and cocooned him with their bodies. The Queen's curse had a strange side-effect, because he could not die as long as Shera was alive, so although damaged, his body would mend in time. His mind however, would take the longest to recover, but eventually, it too would heal.

Aberash arrived aboard the Sea Queen when Jeremy was well enough to talk and listen. She was not there to aid in his recovery, but to help him recover the one he had lost. He could see she was their leader, by her age - which was hardly a gauge to judge anything about these mysterious beings - and the reverence the others paid her.

"How? Why?"

"This goes back millennia," she told him.

Mind speak was still beyond him. Except for Shera, he had a hard time making sense of the other mermaids' thoughts. They came to him as a jumble of voices instead of a conversation.

"We were once all united in service to this world. Mermaids, as you know us, cared for all life that swims. Mankind cared for those that walk upon the land. And the Molytans took care of the winged creatures. We worked in harmony, as the Creator intended it."

"So how did I end up like this?"

"In time, the ideal of equality sours in some minds," she told him sadly. "One being seeks to dominate. They twist the truth and mislead the others."

"Mankind..."

"No," Aberash smiled at the young man. "I understand why you would think so, as things stand in the world, but it was Mankind who resisted temptation the longest, and alas, paid the highest price in the end. It was the Molytan who imagined himself superior because he had the power of flight. He could soar above all others, looking down on everything, so he thought that he should rule."

Aberash began to tell the story...

"Ten lifetimes ago the Earth was a very different place. There was one ocean and one land. The land was vast with hills and valleys, and two great mountains. One marked the rising sun, the other the place where it set, and there flowed two mighty rivers from each of the mountains. One river flowed into the base of the mountains from the ocean and the other down the mountain and across the land. The land was green and fertile, the ocean teemed with life, and the flocks, like clouds, extended for miles, as they migrated from feeding grounds to nesting grounds.

"Maidens were the healers, caring for the life of the sea as well as tending to the wounded or injured, both on land and in the ocean. Mankind cultivated the land and kept creatures in their place. The Molytans were fire and wind, cleared the dead, and made way for new birth, making sure all things followed in succession. From their vantage point in the clouds, they could see when things were out of order and set them right.

"The Molytans were much smaller and thinner than the other two caretakers, with long fragile wings that made walking an awkward task. They had translucent skin through which their life force shone as sunbeams. Although beautiful to look at from a distance, their body heat made all other living things shy away from them as well. They grew jealous of both Mankind and Mermaid for being able to interact with other creatures and each other, starting to believe that because they existed apart from and above all other life forms they must be superior.

"They convinced man and maid that it would be possible to share each other's powers if they went to the Tree of Life – the one where all species had come from – and drank the nectar. So, three emissaries were chosen.

However, the tree was thousands of leagues away, unreachable if any attempted to do so on their own. Mermaid legs were fragile and brittle to walk it alone and she needed man to dig pools along the way to soak their aches away. Furthermore, the tree was also too deep in the jungle for Mankind to find, in fact, the only way to locate the center of the land and the Tree of Life was from high above. But Ehecatl – for that was the Molytan's name – could not reach it on his own either. Due to his delicate wing structure, he needed to leap into the air to attain flight, so he required another tree or launching site to soar, but there were none within range, and of course, he could not stay in the skies indefinitely.

"Thus, Ehecatl guided the other two to the heart of the continent, man carrying him and the mermaid in turns along the way. Man dug pools where the mermaid said there be water, and cut through the dense forest which grew broader as they neared the interior. But eventually, he hacked through the last obstacle and revealed the Tree of Life. It looked insignificant, but that was because they were far off. As they began crossing the clearing, the ground turned to roots, thick and interwoven. Five days later they stood beneath the outstretched branches of the towering tree, its limbs so long and numerous it blotted out the sky.

"While the mermaid was telling Ehecatl that she did not feel right about what they were about to do, the man mindlessly stuck his knife into the tree. He withdrew it at once but a red sap oozed forth. While the other two watched in shock, man licked the fluid from the blade and finding it sweeter than anything he had ever tasted, offered it to his companions. Ehecatl stuck both hands into the liquid which flowed like blood down the trunk and quickly traversed the roots. He would have tasted it as well but he noticed a perplexing reaction on the man. Man's age had doubled in a matter of minutes.

"The Molytan tried to shake off the red ooze but it was too late. It spread over his body and infused his gossamer wings. He flapped and turned, growing exponentially as he tried to free himself from the fluid. His bright and shinning skin became black and leathery.

"The saturated roots shook and the drenched earth split, over and over again, and the sea roared inland to fill the crevices. It was then the mermaid tried to escape but it was too late, the ooze caught up with her as well. A few drops on her feet was all it took to burn her feet and legs so badly, that she plunged into the swirling waters, never to climb out again.

"Ehecatl became the dragon and unleashed a war of revenge against Maiden and Mankind alike," said Aberash as she concluded. "Mermaids lost the ability to live on land for any extended period of time. And men... your life was cut short. Instead of the thousand years you were supposed to experience, you are lucky to last one hundred."

Chapter 9
The Gift of Love

After a year in the care of maidens, Jeremy was at long last healthy again. They strengthened him in mind and body and prepared him for what trials his love for their sister placed in his path. His ordeal was only just beginning and they all knew it.

Aberash gave him a small pocket satchel containing six crystals and explained their purpose. *Aquamarine to reveal your true destiny. Bloodstone to ground and protect you. Hematite will transform negative energy, which is all around you on the Queen's ship, and to oxygenate your blood. Moonstone to help you face your inner demons. Remember always, these are the Queen's greatest weapon against you. Rose Quartz is the love stone; it will bring you peace, and strengthen your communications with Shera. And finally, Emerald, to power the healing and spiritual powers of the other stones. It will give you strength you were not aware you possessed, the strength to survive the Third Split.*

If this is the Queen's ship, what happened? And what is this Third Split you have been mentioning all this time?

Yes, the Sea Queen was built by Rehema's husband for her. But it is yours now as you need it to find Shera. And we need you to find her, because only you can reach her now.

I know that her husband was lost at sea. Is that why she is so bitter? Because she couldn't save him?

I doubt it, since she is the one who sank the ship. But think not about her, rather focus your mind on Shera, and she will come to you.

I see her, in a dark and wet cave. She stands on a rock surrounded by water but it is only ankle deep. She is wearing jewelry, bracelets and a necklace of gold. No! Not jewelry, the gold weighs her down, burns her, and drains her strength. They are chains and shackles.

Yes, this is Sun metal. You men crave it, we maidens abhor it. Where? Where is she?

I do not know. I cannot see or hear anything, save the sound of waves, and the frost of her breath. She is cold, freezing. East. She is east.

You have your heading, sisters. Your Captain cries, EASTWARD HO!

Jeremy watched the maidens climb the shrouds quickly to the yardarms. They had woven cloth from the seaweed which continued to grow and ensnare the ship, and from the cloth, they had made strong and sturdy sails to withstand the full force of a hurricane wind. But they seemed to forget, here there was no wind at all. The sails hung flat from their yardarms.

Aberash reached out. *Ehecatl we have a course. It is time for you to fulfill your promise.*

And as for your promise...

Look to the globe and eye that which you desire.

Ehecatl held the globe, the trio had given him, up to the sun. Red lines connected the rubies, green hues covered the sphere, and blueish shades from the sapphires marked the oceans. Slowly, all the dragon nesting places became clear.

He spread his wings and with a single stroke rose high enough to eclipse the sun for miles around the mountain. As he circled, he gathered energy from the rays on his back. To the humans below, he merely appeared as a spreading storm cloud. They ran for shelter.

How appropriate, he thought.

Ehecatl, Spirit of the Wind, to your promise. Commanded Aberash.

Jeremy observed. *Dragon! Surely, he is nothing more than a myth.*

A year ago, you were sure mermaids were the tales of rum-soaked minds.

The dragon grew in size and power and lightning flashed in the clouds above the mountain. Ehecatl landed

113

atop his home with a thunderous boom that shook trees and rocks from their roots, inhaled deeply, and jammed the entire length of his snout into his den. He forced his head and neck in, now swollen with air and energy. The mountaintop cracked and boulders tumbled down as Ehecatl dug deep, destroying his lair. Roaring loud and long, he expelled a stream of white hot fire down the mountain's inners. The Temple of the Dragon glowed bright, revealing the head, body, tail, and folded wings carved into the mountainside. The granite dragon awoke, and for miles around, thousands witnessed the colossal image writhe and twist the summit in the coils of its body, as it thundered up and down ridges and crevices; threatening to tear itself from the stone and descend upon the terrified humans. Gargantuan boulders pried themselves loose and plummeted to the valley below, some large enough to crush entire villages at once. And did so.

The Earth rumbled in protest of the dragon's might and flames burst from peaks east to west, as it bled its fiery essence, scarring the land beneath. And within scores of mountains, the hearts of dragons, still cocooned in protective crystal shells, beat with life. Beneath the sea, one geyser erupted, shooting steam and scalding mud from the ocean floor to the air above, and within the vent, a tiny crystal glowed.

Ehecatl exhaled all he had stored up over the centuries and did not draw another breath, instead, the world responded with a breath of its own. A gale force wind blew from every corner of the globe and filled the sails of the Sea Queen, at last setting her free from her stagnation.

Rehema, thousands of miles away knew at once that dragons had returned to the world. The Third Split had begun.

What is this Third Split? Questioned Jeremy again from the deck of his ship.

War. Aberash told him simply.

Once they cleared the last of the giant seaweed, Aberash and six of her maidens returned to the sea, on their way to the Mediterranean, as she could not sense Rehema any longer, who seemed to have chosen to cut herself off from her sisters and daughters. Aberash imagined it as the final attempt to keep Shera's whereabouts secret for as long as possible. But despite her attempts to hide and cover, ironically, her curse was now working against her for there was Jeremy, the one who could make direct contact. Lamentably, he was still inexperienced so it was going to be a while before they found and rescued her.

For that very reason, Shreya and Shahira remained aboard the Sea Queen; to improve his abilities, and for his protection, continuing to give him the powder made from the crushed crystals that had brought him back to health, and assembling in the Triad of the Moon to join their powers with his mind to guide them. Their direct bloodline to Shera made their powers combine more readily with his. With Jeremy as the compass point, they sat behind him, each with a hand to his temple. He still could not see Shera but he could feel her and that feeling would grow stronger as they got closer. They left the Equatorial waters, heading southeast across the Atlantic.

Following Aberash's example, Raakel took another group of six and swam southeast. Maidens swam faster than any ship and as soon as Jeremy had a location, she wanted to be there.

They imagined that Rehema might have chained Shera in the cave herself, and perhaps she had done so to ensure secrecy, but that was not to say that she would not have spies and agents close by. Nobody was certain or foresaw what shape the Split would take but knowing her sister, it was prudent to take no chances, for only very few were still alive who had been part or witness to the Second Split.

The First had fallen to myth and legend, even in the world of Maidens. Seeing the carvings and paintings in the Temple of the Dragon had reminded Raakel how horrific war was. Time had made maidens shrewd and they tried to stay clear of such things, for that was the pastime of men. Killing for fun and sport suited their nature now, having forgotten how to care for others and were instead out to amass all they could for themselves. In her six hundred years, she had seen men become kings, kingdoms built into empires, and ultimately seen those empires crumble back into the dust. But she had never imagined that she would see the day when such a conflict would be

116

possible in her world, not over a man, a maiden, and a whale.

Raakel and her maidens kept swimming southeast, teaming up with a pod of whales for a trip around Africa if necessary. She still only had a general direction from Shera's sisters on the ship, which meant they only had a general direction from Jeremy.

As they neared the African coast they came upon three vessels under sail going in the opposite direction. Great despair emanated from one of the craft, a Carrack with two masts and gray square sails. The maidens stopped, unable to get any closer to the cargo ship and its human freight, the weight of shackles and chains on the slaves dragging them down. The seven had been in such a heightened sense for so long that the misery aboard the merchant ship was soul crushing. The other two vessels, one forward and the other aft, were forty-gun men-of-war. Joyous songs rang out from the decks in concert with the pulling of lines and bluffing of sails but it could not mask the fact that each sailor's hands were bloody and their souls dark. Much death was carried in the voices from those ships.

Raakel knew in times such as these, when sorrow drifted far on the wind, and war swords rattled in their scabbards, demanding to be let loose, that the love of two could change the course of the world more easily than a hundred ships of the line.

Jeremy stared at the face of the pale blue moon, having seen it wax and wane many times now, and having followed its trail over thousands of waves. His mermaid crew rejoiced as they flew into the sea, leaving him in solitude. With only a soft light, mild breeze at his back, and pain in his heart to keep him company this night, he did what he habitually did; recall the taste of her in his mind. And that was all he needed, for at once it came to him. Like an invisible hand unfurling a map across the infinite sky, a line bright and true connecting stars, he glimpsed a destination at last.

They leapt like dolphins ahead of the ship, but Raakel and her band being closest to the southern tip of Africa, continued speedily south through the Great White Waters towards the ice. Thankfully, they would not have to go all the way to the huge ice flows of the Antarctic. The waters there were so cold that even maidens feared them. Every living creature had its limit, and that included mermaids.

She turned east once more towards the southernmost part of the Indian Ocean. Thousands of miles away from any land, was a small island, and several miles south of it was the tiniest bit of ice-covered rock that could be called an island. There, entombed in the frigid cave, in golden chains anchored to the wall, Shera hung by her frail arms in icy water barely deep enough to keep her alive. Providentially, the island was volcanic by nature and its internal warmth was the only reason Shera had not yet succumbed.

Jeremy saw her in his mind, and half a world away, he exploded in a fit of rage. His crew tried to calm him down but there was no chance of that happening in the immediate moment. Then Shreya quickly pointed out that his mood was as painful as any torture the Queen could devise, so for Shera's sake, he had to control his temper.

He tried but the long separation, never-ending months at sea and the vast distance yet to travel, were beyond difficult to deal with and he wished the maidens listened to his pleas and brought her to him. But rightly, they pointed out too that the arduous journey such as he proposed, through shark-infested waters, and in her deteriorated condition, would surely kill her. They had her now and she was safe, so he had to be patient. But for the next several months, as he sailed to her, his mind filled with thoughts of vengeance and death.

Raakel sent two maidens to find tools to liberate Shera from her bonds. They returned with hammer and chisel as well as clothes to dress and protect her from the biting wind once she was free from her restraints and the cave. At once Raakel held her close to share body-heat then placed her mouth over Shera's, who immediately reacted with alarm and fear.

Jeremy responded with indignation over the panic he felt emanating from her.

Calm your mind Jeremy, we act for her benefit and healing and you are a large part of it. She can draw from your energy, especially if you are in a positive state. Not only is she sick and aching, but not being able to do what comes as natural as breathing is humiliating as well.

Jeremy closed his eyes and thought of his love, their time together, the warmth of their embrace. The maidens encircled the ship, swimming slowly and deliberately in undulating motions above and then below the surface, each holding a crystal in her left hand, each carrying a different stone linking them, amplifying their essence, projecting their life force through Jeremy and into Shera.

Every day, he held the five crystals Aberash had given him in his right hand and the emerald in his left, absorbing the piercing cold from Shera's worn-out body and replacing it with the warmth of his heart. Regularly, he found himself gasping – mirroring what Shera felt across the ocean – when Raakel stepped into the pool with the frail girl in her arms. Then thankfully, a gradual calmness entered him as Raakel began a deep and rhythmic inhaling as they slowly descended into the gloom and went to rest at the bottom of the dead lava vent. Raakel always wrapped her tail around Shera, her fins fully extended and lovingly enveloping her niece then stroked her from head to feet and down her back. And there they remained for prolonged periods of time.

There was a reason the dragon had not been able to put eyes on her. The lava vent had spouted many centuries ago, and many more after that had been covered over by newer flows. The only access to the cave was from below water and the tube was long and deep. Even without the golden chains which sapped a maiden's strength, Shera would have been trapped there forever.

Jeremy finally understood the curse they were under. While he burnt on the outside, ensnared on the Sea Queen in the Windless Sea, he had felt an icy cold prick in the core of his heart. Now, in commune with Shera once more, he knew there had been a blaze in hers that had kept her from freezing solid. Perhaps because she was naturally gifted and he merely had this thrust upon him, she had felt his pain much more intensely.

He needed no one to tell him that this was far from over. He could feel the Queen's cruel eyes on him, her merciless soul inside him and it fueled his anger, for she was plotting against them further. The mermaids had not rescued him. They had not saved them. It was all a pretext, the Queen craved war. Not just with him, but against Mankind. And for once, he felt something that very few of the mermaids surrounding and helping him could truly sense. There was a bitter darkness that was quickly descending upon them like an endless stormy night. Regardless, he tried to maintain a positive outlook as he sailed towards her.

Now that Shera was fairly improved, Raakel kept her underwater, continuing her restoration. Then one morning, four of the maidens aboard the Sea Queen left, heading west to the South American continent and Jeremy realized that they must be under some orders. What those were and who had given them he had no clue.

While he had been recuperating months ago, they had obstinately stayed with him, especially inside his head. He had felt and heard their thoughts towards him, and those that flowed through him to Shera, just as if they had been whispering in the outer room. But eventually, on a day he could no longer recall, they had withdrawn, returned his privacy, and he had become very much aware that he could only hear and feel Shera. He tilted his head, listening to the hum of the lines in the riggings. A year had passed since that moonlit night when he had reached out across the world's vastness and finally found her.

Awaiting her eventual emergence from the water, the maidens had built a camp and shelter on the leeway side of the island. Shera had left the water three months previously and now, dressed in the heavy gowns and robes her sisters had brought, she was well rested but anxious for Jeremy's arrival. They spent hours inside each other's minds and now she longed for his touch once more.

Raakel said, "I don't know what is so special about men. I tried it once. It was fun but I can live without it."

"That is because you were not in love with him, silly," Shera countered.

"Does that really make a difference?"

"It makes all the different in the world," Shera whispered as the others drew closer to her. They preferred their natural form but in these frigid waters it was unbearably painful hence they spent as much time on land as they could. "His lips are oxygen in my lungs when they touch mine. His hands like liquid moon metal on my skin, powerful, yet soft and yielding. And his body..." Her voice dropped low as she stared at her feet. "Why can't I maintain my form?"

"Try not to concern yourself dear sister, we will see to it that you become well again. This man, he is your world and you are his." Raakel stated rather than asked, as she lifted her chin to look into the verdant eyes. "You will find that it does not matter what form you take as long as you are happy with each other. But we have a surprise for you." She announced with a broad smile. "Something that will make survival in this form so much easier."

On cue, the four mermaids who had left the Sea Queen rose from the ocean and struggled to lift an enormous emerald above their heads. At once the other maidens ran to help them carry the flawless rock and lay it carefully on the beach.

"A gem from the finest waters," said one of the four who had quarried it from the jungles of South America.

The stone was seven-feet long, five wide and without a single blemish. Its color was iridescent seaweed green, which shone and sparkled, and its tone as bright as a full moon, as the sun traversed its four-feet depth as if it were merely a thin sheet of stained glass in a cathedral.

"What is it?" Shera asked as wide-eyed as a child.

"This is your chamber," said Raakel, "we will carve it and fill it with seawater. It will heal and amplify your powers."

The maidens got to work immediately, carefully chipping and carving the massive stone. They worked for weeks, turning the block into a circle and a cup with swirls spiraling inwards as they inlaid other gems and crystals into the sides. They engraved intricate star patterns and constellations, and made a relief of Usea Maya in its center on both sides. When completed, they had turned the shapeless mass into an upturned nautilus, the circled end completely enclosed. Inside, it curled into a hidden chamber, also etched with special markings. Their idea, a means to transform her into the image of what she had once been. She could enter through the cup-like end and lounge with her head and arms out. The nautilus could only be filled halfway, leaving plenty of breathing room inside the shell, and as sunlight shone through its translucency, she appeared to have a tail and fins once more.

Shera loved it, and dove in as soon as it was filled. The water was naturally cold but she hardly noticed. Sun rays refracted and reflected through the walls around the nautilus and her body's energy levels quickly warmed the liquid. It also raised her spirits, and she felt happier than she had been in a long time. She splashed in the tub and played happily underwater then emerged and rested her arms on the rim, gazing lovingly out to sea, focusing her eyes on a faint image as it appeared far off in the horizon. A tiny ship with green sails had just reached the South Indian Ocean. Jeremy had arrived.

My love, at last you have come.

"I am here," Jeremy said standing next to the nautilus. "Is there something wrong? Why don't you speak to me?"

I am speaking to you, and only you. No one else can hear. My sisters made this tub to return as many of my powers as is possible.

"Splendid!" Seeing a tail through the emerald, he excitedly looked in. Disappointment filled him instantly as he saw her legs. "What is this trickery? They are lying to you. They have not returned you to your natural form. They have not broken the Queen's curse."

No, she admitted. *No one can, but while in here, I am as close to what I once was as can be.*

This makes you happy. Jeremy could not hide his frustration.

Not happy, content. No one, but the Queen, can return us to our former selves but at least I am not cut off from my sisters. And now you are here, we can go somewhere, far from the madness, and be happy. That is all I want. To put the sorrow behind us and live.

125

"You know perfectly well the Queen is not letting us go that easily because you can feel her machinations too. She is merely waiting for your sisters to depart, to leave you defenseless. Then she will strike again." Jeremy slammed his fist against the side of the nautilus. "And this fancy tub is not going to protect you."

But in here I can protect you. Shera gazed at Jeremy. Two years of agony had changed him. This was not the same kind-hearted man who had taken a young boy to sea so he could provide for his family. Not the same man who had fashioned a raft in the height of a killer storm to save that boy. Not the same man who would have gladly lain down on a sword to save her. New things brewed inside him, some dark and dangerous.

He lifted her from the tub and held her naked body to his. It was this feeling of full arms that he had hankered for. Steam vapors rose around her and he quickly draped his cloak over her back and shoulders then swung her up and she wrapped her arms around his neck. Turning, he carried her up the gangplank to his quarters. Dropping her gently onto their bed, he peeled back the cloak to gaze at her then closed his eyes for a second and opened them again; making sure she was no figment of his imagination.

She reached up and pulled him down. Finally, here they were, back in each other's arms. In semi-crazed movements, he ripped the shirt from his body and kicked the pants off hastily. Through the burning of skin and freezing of blood, both had dreamt of only one thing, thirsting for this moment to return even during every hurt and torment. And in that instant, Shera recognized the

126

man she loved. Beyond this bed, outside of this time, he would forever be changed. But here, he returned to the loving caring man she longed for, had waited for, and knew he still was deep within his soul. She would help him find him again.

Under Jeremy's instructions, the maidens helped prepare the ship for sailing home. They cleared the back room in the Captain's quarters then removed windows and shutters, and using the mizzen-mast halyard, lifted and swung the emerald nautilus into the cabin. When Jeremy found green paint in the ship's store that vaguely matched Shera's eyes, he scraped Sea Queen from the stern and renamed her The Emerald Lady.

Maidens stood back and nodded approval then loaded four chests with the surplus cuttings from the nautilus.

The Emerald Lady's first port of call was at the Cape of Good Hope. There, Jeremy traded a chest of emeralds for a dozen cannons of various poundage and size and hired a crew of mostly Africans and several Europeans before setting out for the Americas. All but one maiden left to rejoin Aberash in her Mediterranean citadel. Shahira remained, looking like a tall Indian sailor, to help protect the pair as only she could.

In the nautilus, Shera's powers were as strong as any other maiden's, but out of it she was noticeably weaker. She longed to return to the fair waters of the Caribbean or the safety of the South Pacific but that would be dangerous, for those were maiden territories. Jeremy suggested they settle off the coast of North America, in the southern waters.

Chapter 10
The Rebels

Raanan had always lived a sheltered life, never venturing far from the sanctuary of Usea Maya. This had promoted a youthful appearance, fresh bright brown eyes almost as light as amber and matching skin tone. It also gave her an outlook on the world to match her personality and equally, her devotion to the Queen was absolute.

In turn, the Rehema protected all who stayed close-by from the outside world, as in the last three hundred years men had taken to the seas in ever-growing numbers and larger ships. For safety, and trying to avert discovery, she and those she commanded had frequently lured ships into storms and onto the rocks, destroying them swiftly. Now, Maidens who had once been considered a blessing to sailors had become Mermaids, the source of dread among those who harvested the seas.

What her followers were not aware of was that their beloved Queen had done much to instill distrust and fear in the younger maidens, most of whom had never seen a human. She had a vast collection of horror accounts and shared memories of men who had captured maidens in their nets and because of their great beauty had taken them to land and made them their wives. Or stories of maidens who for one reason or another had become involved in the affairs of men, and once their powers were discovered had either been exploited or put to the fire as witches.

Rehema had been very successful in segregating her people and keeping them confined within the waters of Usea Maya, as she regularly told them, "for your own good." So now, she used Shera's story as a good example of a cautionary tale to the dangers of men. Her banishment and torment would curtail others who were considering venturing out through fear. And her power would be absolute.

Raanan, open your eyes and see for yourself.

Aberash! The Queen has told us of your treachery. You have released our enemy upon us. Why?

Great mistakes have been made in the past. To continue on the same path is to walk into ruin. Our sister is leading you into darkness. Open your eyes. See the truth for yourself.

The maidens vacated the throne room and the Queen was unusually alone in the main pool in the center of the chamber. She was quiet, brooding, holding the silver scepter in hand, running her fingers along the shaft, tracing the ancient symbols of elements and constellations. Her reflection in the large globe on top was something she always admired, so she studied the spot where she stood gazing at the Tree of Life growing from her mouth and spread between her eyes. Her face contained the world.

Suddenly, she knew she was not alone anymore. "So, sister, have you come to fight for my scepter, MY Throne, MY POWER?"

Aberash rose slowly from a nearby pool and stepped onto the hard stone. White hair flowing around her, she stopped at the edge of the main pool across from Rehema. "This is not about any of those things, it is about you. What happened to you, my sister? When mother chose me to lead, I chose you. You were merciful then and I knew you would lead us on the righteous path. Where did that path split? When did you slip into the shadow? What feeds this madness within you?"

Rehema transformed, stepped out of the pool, and locked her eyes on her sister as she slowly approached her. "So, do you want the power you passed on five hundred years ago? Now that I have done all the work to ensure our security, you think you can walk in here and take over?"

"All you have done will be undone. We have rescued the man and freed your daughter. Power gained

131

through fear and intimidation is the path to tyranny and it will not last."

"You want MY power. THEN TAKE IT!" Rehema swung the heavy silver scepter and struck the maiden on the left temple, who twisted and crumbled to the ground, her white hair turning to dirty blonde and a large rivulet of blood filling the grooves on the floor. Rehema's face softened for a moment at Raanan's gentle features, but wasting no time, she immediately sent a mental link throughout the world of Aberash standing over the fallen maiden. *Sisters, find Aberash. Do not let her get away with this.*

The undersea kingdom churned and maidens around the globe became horrified and torn between those who simply believed, those who did not, and the most dangerous, those who wished to profit.

Aberash, sitting in her pool with Raakel and Shreya, shook her head sadly. "Our poor sister, even I did not think she was this far astray."

"Never has a maiden killed another maiden. We must go to Usea Maya and take control now," insisted Shreya.

"Yes. Before the situation gets any worse," agreed Raakel.

"It is already too late for that," Aberash lamented, "Rehema has far more under her power than just maidens. She plans to put them to use against us and each other. What we must do is build allegiances while we still have the time."

132

☠   ☠   ☠

Rehema arrived in Boston as Regina Cutter-Smythe, the great granddaughter of Davin Cutter, sole heiress to the Cutter Ship Builders. The company had been operating under various leaderships and now the fifty-year-old woman was there to take control. She met with town officials in a backroom of the Old South Meeting House where her portrait hung.

"You look remarkably like your Great-Grandmother Mrs. Rehema Cutter," observed Gregory Hewes.

There was not another line on her face that was not portrayed in the portrait, her eyes and hair as radiant as ever. If the smoky air of the Meeting House had not darkened the oils of the painting one might have mistaken it for a mirror.

"The result of strong families I venture, Sir." That was all Rehema said about the subject. Then she discussed business matters with the four men, smiling and charming her way into their hearts and minds. And without them realizing it, she whipped them into a froth over three ships docked at the Griffin's wharf, which were loaded with the latest source of contention between the Crown and the Colonists, tea. Or more to the fact, taxes due on the shipment of leaves from the East India Shipping Company.

For Rehema was an expert at getting men to do as she wished, having already led both English and French into bloody sea battles only a few years previously when she became incensed at their ships navigating far too close to her home waters. She showed up in the courts of both kingdoms to implant the notion of superiority and invincibility in their minds. Making whatever differences they had unsolvable without bloodshed, and a good amount of it. Now, she would stir the pot in the colonies. It was the first of December 1773, and the cold temperatures made men more rigid than usual in their dealing with the English government.

Jeremy stopped in the Caribbean to resupply the Emerald Lady and release his crew of Africans, who had no desire to travel to the Americas, rather seeking to get work on an East India ship heading back to Africa or the Orient. He left them at Hispaniola and attempted to hire some Spaniards. Presently, a rumor began circulating among the crews that the ship sailed under the influences of magic. Most men said it was favorable, but magic just the same. Others claimed Jeremy was under the dark powers of a witch, for they had been told that voices were regularly heard in his quarters when there should not be any. And often, the Captain seemed lost in a dream, almost as if in a trance. Not only that, but the boatswain had a strange habit of diving from the poop-deck in the middle of the night. He was gone for hours, but always back onboard in the morning. Dressed in the traditional long silk coat and slacks made it hard to believe that he could swim fast enough to keep up with a ship under sail.

After a few days in port, Jeremy started thinking that he would not find a replacement crew any time soon, as neither the French nor Spanish were interested in signing onto the Emerald Lady. She had no history, no one had heard of her, yet she was not newly built. That was obvious from her look. Everything about his ship was queer.

Jeremy was becoming agitated; he wanted to get underway as soon as possible. Shera noticed that his mood swung like a pendulum. He was only calm within his quarters with her and always fully outraged on deck and that added to the difficulty of hiring a crew. Shera rarely left the nautilus, except to sleep with Jeremy and spent even less time on deck. She only went there when Jeremy or Shahira took the last watch, never when any of the other men were out of quarters.

Annoyed with the stalemate situation, Shahira went to the taverns one night and came back with thirty-four men ready to toe the line.

Jeremy asked, "How were you so successful? What made these men so agreeable?"

"I am able to see what motivates men, and offer it to them," Shahira told him. "Mostly, these men have a desire to leave this island, and are not concerned with the how or where of their journey. My question to you is this, what is your motivation to get underway again?"

"These waters be not safe for Shera. Surely, you feel it as well."

"Know this Jeremy Simmons," she said sternly, "no waters are a safe haven for Shera. Nor should you feel safe, either on water or dry land. Undoubtedly, the Queen still hunts you, but that does not essentially mean she is chasing you. Be on guard against your plans and thoughts; make sure they are of YOUR own doing."

Shahira had mixed feelings about Jeremy. His heart was torn between consuming love for her sister and raging desire for revenge. Both powerful emotions and each carrying dire consequences when left to run wild in the mind, and the results total disaster if controlled by another. Jeremy was hardly aware of the strength and extent of maidens' dominance over the minds of men. She was afraid to tell him for fear that he would rebel against all maidens, not just the Queen.

December twelfth. Rehema was in the backroom once more meeting with the colonial leaders. She told them she was thinking of closing the boatyard. "There are too many tariffs from the Crown. I think I should move to France."

"Madam, please, I beg you to reconsider," Mr. Hewes implored.

"But if you let them unload that shipment of tea by the Crown's puppet, there will be no end to the amount of taxes I will be charged."

"We can stop this," insisted Gregory Hewes. His fear of losing her business in the town was only surpassed by his desire for her. And that desire grew every time he saw her. "We will go to the Harbor Master and demand he order the ships out of port."

"If you really want to send the Crown a message about taxes, you would burn the Indiamans."

"Surely, Madam, this is a poorly conceived joke. Boston will be besieged by Redcoats. We have a tenuous peace, at best."

Rehema commanded, "Cowardice does not ensure peace, only further encroachments on one's sovereignty."

They left to contemplate her proposition and entered the riotous meeting hall. While some demanded sterner action, fearing the loss of income from her shipbuilding business, others won out with putting pressure on the Harbor Master. Meanwhile, Rehema was already paying the man a visit, ensuring he played his part in her plot. A simple suggestion would do for him.

Stand fast, keep to your duties.

Rehema glanced at her portrait on the wall. She would have been insulted to be relegated to the backroom if she had not known that two hundred years ago this had been the only room in the Meeting House. How foolish to have believed that the love of a man was worth giving up her power for. She had almost lost everything for nights of passion, which had not been that many anyway as he was always away at sea, where she should have been... The shouts from the hall merged with her memories. Yes, men's hearts were strong and burnt with desire, but their will was weak and their minds malleable. Davin Cutter had been no different.

His portrait hung next to hers and she had a mind to smash it. The great shipbuilder. He was nothing! Would have been nothing, if it had not been for her. His hull designs only a slight improvement over the oak and tar of the day. She had recommended he build ships out of pine. The wood's oil made it naturally water resistant, so they were lighter, faster, and required less time cleaning and tarring. And naturally, she had not disclosed the most important reason for suggesting the use of pine. It was less damaging to the seas than tar.

He made several runs in the time it took others to make one. His shipping business flourished. His reward for her? He married her. Taking her from the home where she had been Queen and turned her into his slave. Wisely, she kept her true nature from him, but she was a sea creature first and foremost so it did not take her long to discover a brackish pool deep in the woods surrounding their house and she made sure to return to the ocean waters every full moon. She thought she was happy. Thought she was in love. Thought he loved her.

Rehema knew the people of Boston mistrusted her. Oh, the men were more than delighted to be in her presence, as men usually are in the company of beautiful women. But the women were jealous, wealthy and common alike, as most often are when meeting another distinctly far above their stature. She did not have to read minds to know what all thought of her and her three hand-maidens, most were simply wise enough to keep it amongst themselves. Still, that did not deter the constant whispers.

"Where did they come from?"

"I do not recall seeing them onboard during the crossing."

However, not all females were suspicious. Many of the local young girls sat for hours in her house listening to accounts concerning the European courts. Rehema was regal and she carried herself as such, although she made no claim to any throne, and everyone could see it, sensing mystery. But her hand-maids intrigued them the most, especially the two negroes. They were not like the ones they knew, free or slave, their skin was black but shone like none they had ever encountered. Their hair thick and braided like well-worked rope, long and soft to the touch. The third hand-maiden spoke with an accent that none could place; some said it was from a Nordic land.

Questions and rumors surrounded them but no one voiced them aloud as an accusation of such magnitude was too damning, but they certainly thought it. They determined that she must be a witch but decided to be civil so not to fall into disfavor. Nonetheless, all kept their distance and watched her every move.

As years passed, the shipyard became a main source of income in Boston and supported multiple of industries, Davin's and Rehema's influence grew, and their interests became Boston's concerns. They shaped politics and business alike and Davin built a larger house on the hill overlooking the yard and harbor. Large parties and important dinners were held for every occasion, distinguished gentlemen and ladies from all colonies and those visiting from the continent attended. More servants were needed. More rumors flourished. And while the life of a sea captain showed on his face, she remained youthful and fair; more than any other woman in the colonies, privileged or not.

And there was talk of a pallor befalling the house. Nights of the full moon when all inside took to bed and a heavy sleep crept over them. In the markets, servants whispered that they could not wake until noon the following day. On occasion, baking bread was found burnt through. Smoke from the ovens not enough to rouse the scullery maids in the next room. There was haziness, lots of talk about the house, its mistress and her hand-maidens. Then came the night of the Blood Moon.

Davin returned early that year, an accident having cut his trip short. When he arrived home, his wife was missing, and the servants quickly told him that she often took walks in the wood. Following her trail in silence to surprise her, he was brought to a sudden halt as he espied her frolicking naked in the moonlight with her three hand-maids. Rehema should have sensed his presence but she was so overjoyed that she heard nothing and he watched in shock as his wife went from woman to mermaid and back again when she exited the pool.

"What witchery is this?" He confronted her the next morning.

"It is not a trick of the devil, it is what I am. We have always existed, as has man, been a companion and aid," she tried to explain. "And I have often been there to aid you on your voyages. Guided your helmsmen to calm seas."

But as always, men condemn what they cannot comprehend, "you will burn, witch! Just like your cohorts!"

As soon as he announced that he had already placed her hand-maidens in chains, spirited them away and secretly sent to Salem to stand trial as witches, she knew he would not heed her pleas and that like them, she stood no chance. Seemingly, he and the male servants he could trust had poured wine into them to make their transportation event-free, as he, like everyone else, believed that witches had extraordinary strength and power. This, ironically, was not wrong, except that they were no witches. The truth was that maidens were unfamiliar with alcohol. It dulled their minds and made them sleep.

Davin told the driver, another servant, "witches cannot abide wine; it is the drink of Our Lord. And be sure to wait for me, I will be there as soon as I take care of the ring leader."

It was then Rehema cursed him and wished to high heaven that she was indeed a witch. But realizing he had her trapped and alone, she used the power she could to run for her life, and the townspeople never saw her again.

The maidens did not wake until they were in the minister's house in Salem, finding themselves gagged and hands and feet tied to poles. The gags clearly necessary to prevent them from casting spells on the men holding the trial; held in secret to protect the good name of Cutter.

There were just three men present, Davin Cutter, Reverend McPeters, and the Inquisitor, who administered the beatings, although, Davin's account was all that was required to condemn the women. What was missing from his testimony was his wife's involvement, as being married to a witch was almost as bad as being one. But that, he was in no hurry to impart with anyone lest they summarily got rid of him too. Hence, throughout proceedings, he requested the women remain gagged to diminish their cursing capabilities. The Inquisitor, who seemed to be rather attached to his craft and deriving great pleasure from it, told them to nod their confession to witchcraft. They refused. He whipped and clubbed them until he ran out of might but they never conceded. Davin pointed at them, feeling revolted by the sight, just further proof of their sins.

The three men dragged the bloody and broken women still tied to the posts out into the minister's courtyard then stood them in three of the apertures on the scorched cobblestones, hastily covered the bases with thicket and kindling and drenched the women with oils. The minister said words, condemning them, claimed his own righteousness and offered God's mercy. The Inquisitor laid a torch to each mound of wood with a twisted smile and then watched stupefied as the women transformed and burnt. An unholy screech awoke the good people of Salem.

Davin Cutter was quick to make up a story, Rehema had taken ill and he was taking her to the finest medical institutions in Europe. The Sea Queen set sail the next day with a skeleton crew, twelve able-bodied men. It was October 31, 1585. But she would not find her way through the Fall storms as she had done before. The helmsman was put on a bad course from the start and sailed directly into a late season hurricane.

Winds shredded the sails on their yardarms and waves battered the ship and spun her around, like a child's toy in a bathtub. Then, a single wave crashed onto the deck and swept it clear of her crew. Captain Davin Cutter was left alone. And Rehema, in her maiden form. Her tail coiled thrice beneath her for support as she towered above him and her eyes blazed like fire and burnt straight into his soul. Then she transformed into her human shape before the terrified sea captain.

I loved you. Even taking on this repulsive form to please you. I allowed myself to become barren, and as repayment, you threatened me with fire. And my sisters, who did nothing but wait on you, were beaten, tied to stakes and burnt to ash. I heard their screams of anguish, felt their pain, the heat of death crawl up their skin. But now, I shall have my revenge. I will see you and your precious ship on the bottom for all time to come.

Rehema dove back into the stormy sea, and as she did, a wave like a mountain raced towards the ship. Davin ran for the port side but the water struck the ship's starboard at mid-length and punched through. Davin went crashing across the deck and was tossed down the hatch. The Sea Queen flooded quickly and was dragged to the bottom. Captain and crew lost.

Shaking memories away, Rehema felt her old ship approaching; Jeremy was drawn to her. She smiled at her own reflection. How could he not be? Men were so easy to manipulate. The colonists sent a delegation to the Harbor Master and she made sure he received her message loud and clear.

Stand fast Master Boon.

Gregory Hewes spoke for the others, "Harbor Master, Mr. William Boon, sir. We represent the people of this city of Boston, colony of Massachusetts. As duly appointed men thereof, and with powers to speak on all matters concerning the business with and for the Colony, I hereby charge you to release these ships from harbor with their full cargo. We hereby reject and refute any and all charges set forth against this Colony."

"You may do what you wish with the cargo," William Boon agreed, "dump the lot into the sea for all I care. But having reached its destination intact and whole, His Majesty is entitled to His tariff." He would hear no more from the delegation and closed his door.

His Majesty! This is but a dog begging at his master's table. Lay hands on him and show all you are not the type to be trifled with, Mr. Hewes.

Jeremy felt Rehema's presence as the Emerald Lady entered the harbor. Shera and Shahira could feel it too.

Jeremy, this is a mistake. We should leave here.

I will free you of this curse.

And I think this is a trap, my love.

Listen to her, Jeremy. And if you feel the Queen's presence then she knows you are here too and nothing can be gained by this.

Jeremy sailed past four British Men-of-war anchored in the harbor then saw two more making towards Boston from the North. He imagined they were preparing for winter quarters. But it did feel disturbingly ominous, as if the gray skies were descending around them. And as much as he knew that the right thing to do was to listen to Shera and her sister, to come about and head for safe waters again, he could not give the order. The Queen was here. He would make her retract the curse.

Shahira broke his concentration, standing beside him as the crew docked the ship. "Exactly how do you plan to do that?"

"I'm not sure yet," Jeremy confessed. He had been so preoccupied with getting there that he had not thought about what he would do once he reached the destination. He drew his cutlass, "She will either remove the curse from our heads, or I will remove her head from her shoulders."

Shahira was shocked by his impulsiveness. "Oh, that should work. But are you sure you will recognize her?"

"Yes, of course, how could I ever forget that face?"

"You are assuming she took the same form as at the trial," Shahira warned him, "there is more to this transformation then just growing legs. She can appear older, younger, an African man, a Spanish lady. There is no telling. And there is no telling what she has in mind for you."

After hearing Shahira tell him that she would be of no use to him against the Queen, as she could not detect Rehema in human form as she evidently did not wish to reveal herself, Jeremy decided to go ashore alone. Telling her in response that it was better if she stayed with her sister until the bloody deed was done anyway. He would feel more confident knowing that Shera was protected.

Shera tried once more to plead with him to alter his course. *No matter what she has done to me, to us, you cannot kill the Queen.*

Your sister thinks she can die. And it will remove the curse.

It will. But you can't kill the Queen.

We will see about that.

You can't kill my mother.

Your MOTHER?

Yes. Did you not know? You know everything about me.

He stared at her for a moment. *I guess I did. And that is what makes this punishment so much harsher. She is your mother; does she not have any empathy?*

Jeremy was snapped out of his commune as he stood on the pier. An angry mob approached, two long lines of colonist dressed as Indians marching his way. The first man who reached him had a torch held high in his right hand and a hatchet in his left.

"Friend or Foe?" Gregory Hewes demanded.

"Not a hard choice to make when outnumbered hundreds to one," Jeremy told him. "You will find no quarrel with me."

"Then, friend, join us," commanded Hewes. "We go to repeal the Crown's Tea Tax."

"You appear to be well bodied for your task and I have pressing matters of my own in town." Jeremy stepped aside and the mob moved on. *More of Your Mother's handy-work, no doubt.*

NO DOUBT. NONE. Both sisters' thoughts rang loud in his head. Then Jeremy stopped and turned around when the commotion started.

Aboard the three ships, at the end of the dock, the mob was in a frenzy, smashing holes in the crates with their hatchets and tomahawks, and throwing them overboard. Whooping and hollering like Indians, the colonists spent hours throwing the tea crates into the harbor. The Men-of-war fired no shot nor sent any troops to the aid of the merchant vessels. He hoped the mob did not get out of hand, or close to his ship. But he knew Shahira and Shera could deter any incursion.

Chapter 11
The Pain of Love

Jeremy returned to his ship next morning, the streets
humming with the success of the destroyed tea in the
Boston Harbor. And he noticed the British troops taking to
the long boats and rowing to shore.

"Loosen the lines, hoist all sails, let's pray there is
wind enough to remove ourselves from this madness,"
Jeremy told Shahira.

She piped the orders, calling all hands-on deck and
the ship had already turned from the dock by the time the
first contingency of troops arrived on shore. Without
warning, a Man-of-war maneuvered itself into their path.
Jeremy spun the wheel hard to port trying to avoid it, just

as the HMS Kellem fired a warning shot across her bow. The cannon ball fired with only half a load, so splashing harmlessly in the water twenty yards from The Emerald Lady.

Jeremy knew that with only a dozen cannons and a little more than twice as many men on board, they were no match for one Man-of-war, and there were five more waiting if they managed to make it past the first. He ordered his men to stand down and prepare to be boarded. The HMS Kellem came alongside and boarding planks extended swiftly over the gap. Both ships dropped anchors and tied lines to the deck cleats. A complement of marines boarded The Emerald Lady forward and aft and rounded up the crew, including Shahira dressed as a lascar. Shera on the other hand, prevented the marines from entering the Captain's quarters by implanting the notion that they had just left the cabin.

Jeremy was taken aboard the Kellem. "To what may I owe the honor of His Majesty's interest?" he queried.

"You are the Captain of the, ah, Emerald Lady, Mister..."

"Jeremy Simmons, Sir. Formerly Midshipman in His Majesty Naval Service. Retired."

The tall white haired and bearded Captain was not impressed. "You should have stayed retired from the sea, Sir."

"Yes," agreed Jeremy cordially, "but like all seadogs, I have salt water in my veins."

"Well, that brings us to our business here today. I am going to wring that salt water out of you from the Main's yardarm," the Captain told him belligerently.

"ON WHAT CHARGES, SIR!?" Jeremy demanded incredulously.

"You are aware of the raid and destruction of the tea crates on board the merchant ships last night," insinuated the Captain.

"I took no part in those actions," insisted Jeremy. "I was in town. Searching for a person to settle a debt owed me. You can query more than a dozen people who know of my exact whereabouts last eve. Having not found said person, I moved on. Now, I sail in pursuit of that goal."

"You are not being charged with the destruction of aforementioned property, Mr. Simmons. Those treacherous dogs shall be hunted down and dealt with accordingly," the Captain sneered. "No sir, you are charged with piracy. An offense which allows me to hang you on the spot. Because, while the ships were being pilfered for their cargo of tea, you took liberty of one of their cashboxes. Do you not recognize your booty?" The Captain threw off a tarp from a large chest of gold coins.

"I have never seen that before!"

"Feast your eyes then," ordered the Captain, "and while you are at it, glimpse your crew, to preview your fate."

Jeremy looked back to the Emerald Lady. All his men were hoisted up the yardarms and hung high above the deck, each kicking and twisting as they painfully choked to death. His gaze ran over each one quickly, noticing with relief that Shahira was not among them.

When the last man finally stopped moving and all swayed silently in the wind, the Captain added, "Do not worry, you will be dropped a proper length, and I will enjoy hearing your neck snap."

Jeremy stood on the Forecastle; hands tied behind his back, a noose around his neck, and the other end of the rope attached halfway up the bowsprit. Two sailors held his arms as he walked up the plank to the railing. *Shera, don't watch this.* His mind was silent but he felt her there.

"Do you have any inspiring parting words you would like to leave this world?"

"I would not begrudge this as I do if it was going to kill me outright, rather than hurt a lot, and for a long time."

One of the sailors slid something long and hard into his boot. *You are going to need this later.*

Shahira?

He became weightless for a moment then started down and away from the ship. Shahira had almost certainly pushed him off because no one else would have been concerned on where and when he would land or what he should hit. Still, it happened too fast, giving him no time to close his eyes. The blue sea rushed up towards him then with a loud crack it all stopped.

Fire exploded in Shera's neck and breathing became impossible. She could not feel her hands, her feet, or her body. Her mind swam as her head swayed freely back and forth and the blue sparkling water made her dizzy. She was ill.

The ship's bell sounded and the sailor on the forecastle deck announced, "I will climb out and cut him loose. Let the sea claim his soul."

"No, we will send a long boat to retrieve his body," said a midshipman standing at the Captain's side. "He will be buried before sundown."

Mother, was all this necessary? You killed your sister, and now drive these people to the brink of war. Is it for vengeance on an ancient raised ship, or because we disobeyed you and freed innocent prisoners?

Shahira, my child, you have no idea what is going on here. This is more than just an act of vengeance; I must stop these men from further incursions into our realm. They have forgotten their place and purpose in this world, destroyed their domain and they will do the same to ours. Join with your Queen, and we will end the terror of men once and for all. And if you really cared for your sister, you would have left them where I did, burning hot and freezing cold. But at least they had each other. Now, you have left her with nothing.

A long boat positioned itself beneath Jeremy's swaying body and a sailor climbed out on the bowsprit to cut the rope holding him aloft. The sailors caught him and laid him on a heavy canvas tarp then started to wrap his body.

One of the sailors said, "Close his eyes, I cannot stand the way he is looking at me. I swear he is still with us."

An older sailor threw the top part of the dingy canvas over his head. "There, he is not looking at anyone now. Fold that bottom piece up and let us get him rolled and tied. Alive or dead, he is going in the ground when we reach shore."

Shera lay in the nautilus in darkness, hearing the bodies of the crew splashing into the water, disposed of in the outgoing tide. As pirates, the poor souls were not afforded a proper burial, merely discarded as trash over the side. Each body having been run through from stomach to chest with a cutlass so as to send it straight to Davey Jones' Locker. No one wanted the bodies washing ashore.

Each splash was a painful slap in Shera's face and when the last passed she found herself alone. Shahira was aboard the British Man-of-war heading out to sea, trying to track their mother, who was still disguised among the sailors. Rehema could not hold form for much longer, as the full moon would soon rise and she had to return to the sea. Both would, and then they would have her.

But Shera could not think about her sister or mother, she had to concentrate on Jeremy, but as she did, at first, she felt nothing, her mind a morass of blackness. Then she reached out to him through the ache which lingered on her neck. *I feel your pain. Do you feel mine?*

I do.

Where are you? I can't see you. I can't feel anything but pain.

I am not in pain anymore. It was but a moment then it was gone. But I feel yours, my dearest, I see you suffer. I cannot move, my neck is broken clean.

My love, I can fix that. Just concentrate on me, think only of my body.

That is not hard to do.

Shera placed one hand on her chin and the other at back of her head, and began to chant and sing softly as moonlight rose across the cabin. The marines, those who had placed Jeremy in his grave and were now stationed onboard, heard the strange sound reverberating below deck. They glanced at each other, it was strange and jarring, raising the hair on the back of their necks, so they pretended they heard nothing.

Slowly, moonbeams crept through the cabin windows and over Shera. She began to glow and sing aloud, building up to a crescendo. Then abruptly, she warned. *This is going to hurt, my love.* Then without further ado, she yanked her head quickly and violently from side to side.

A loud cracking sound spread on deck, followed by a woman's scream then another resounding snap and a second scream, both eerily amplified in the cold December air.

Shera had snapped her neck and reset it before death could get hold of her, but not before pain did. Then cautiously, she climbed out from her tub, walked out of the Captain's quarters, and with crimson hair streaming down her body, she made her way on deck as a soft haze rose from her shimmering skin under the moon. She needed its full power to heal Jeremy.

Piercing pain shot down his neck as he felt it being broken yet again and then forcibly returning to its right position. Slowly, sensation returned to his hands, then arms, down his torso, and he found he could breathe again. Next, his legs twitched and it spread all the way down to his feet. At once he wriggled and twisted until he could reach the knife Shahira had slipped into his boot. Patiently, he cut his legs loose then flipped the blade upside down and sawed off his wrist bindings.

Once his hands were free from constrains, he proceeded to liberate himself from the enfolding shroud. Lying still for a few seconds, he knew instantly that he would have to dig quite a way to reach the top. Pushing against the dirt, he realized that the looser soil was the quickest way out. Thus, he dug upwards with his hands and knife, around his back, even as his neck became an intense ball of fire, and as soon as he had some wiggle room, he cut a long strip of canvas and wrapped and tied it around his neck like a collar for added support.

The two marines – the first of the Emerald Lady's new crew – became mesmerized at the sight of Shera standing in the moonlight. And as she persisted with her exquisite song, Jeremy made his way from the church cemetery to the wharf, and was soon joined by others who had also heard the call and responded. Thirty-three men, colonists and British sailors alike, laborers in every kind of servitude, black and white, heard and obeyed. Jeremy staggered on, knowing that these men were not responding as slaves to their master, but as those who had a profound need and an inexplicable desire that had to be satisfied. She offered them something that was missing from their lives; she offered them peace.

The Harbor Master noticed men taking to boats and rowing to the Emerald Lady moored in the harbor, also noticing that the British soldiers on watch, who were under orders to prevent anyone from leaving, made no attempt to halt them. One of the men however struck him with terror, Captain Jeremy Simmons, whom he had seen hanged. With great interest and curiosity, he continued watching through his spyglass as a strange woman welcomed the Captain onboard. He checked in his book quickly, yes, the Emerald Lady was listed as a pirate ship to be sold at the next auction, as was customary as soon as her crew had been disposed of.

The two marines were wide-eyed at the sight of Jeremy, and becoming aware of their shocked countenances, he told Shera, "perhaps you should go put some clothes on while, I address the men."

Shera returned to the Captain's Quarters and quickly got to finding a suitable outfit. She dug under piles of cloth then stared at something she had never worn before. Perhaps a little risqué but there was cause to celebrate, they had once again escaped Rehema's clutches. Feeling daring, she grabbed the red silk and lace bodice with black leather insets to support her bosom. Then she slipped into a matching lace petticoat and wide layered skirt of fine satin. Glancing in the mirror, she tightened the accompanying black leather belt and bra. Silk stockings and leather boots completed the outfit and protected her feet. Now, it felt a little constricting and unnatural but at least offered warmth and protection from the cold night air if she were to walk about the ship. Then she rejoined Jeremy on deck. He had just stopped in front of the two marines again while the other men stood at attention.

"How do I know you two gentlemen?" Jeremy enquired, as he pushed one of their chins up to close the open mouth.

"I am Henry Irons, Captain." The older man stated. "It be my face ye last looked upon before going to ground."

"Does that trouble you, Mister Irons?" Jeremy asked as he studied the face; it was scarred from battles and hardened from years at sea but the eyes were sharp, full of wisdom and caring. "Speak smartly now, we do not have much time to make use of this tide."

"It be this, Sir. Is this ship under a curse?"

"Aye." Chimed the younger marine, a man of Jeremy's age, still fair as if the sailor's existence was his lot in life.

Irons looked crossly at Sam Brantley and continued, "I thought you were falsely accused and executed at first. But only a man in league with the Devil and under subjection to a witch, many pardons Ma'am, can return from the dead to take command of his ship. Is this not so? Before you answer, know this, it was hours before I laid you in the ground myself."

"Verily," Jeremy answered, took hold of Shera's hand tenderly, and contemplated how much he should tell the two.

Tell them all. They have a right to know what life they would choose.

Not all men think and believe alike. Jeremy disagreed.

Men are all the same. The differences are in your eyes and in your tongue. All men can accept the truth when plainly spoken.

"Justice can never be killed, nor the truth stay buried," Jeremy told the two men. "You heard me tell your Captain that I served in His Majesty's Service. It was during the war with the French that I served with a just and honest Captain. We gave quarters to the enemy when right to do so and exacted no undo malice upon them. That is what brought me to these waters."

"You seem to me to be a man of honor and distinction," Irons said, "So how tells it you and Milady comes under this Devil's spell?"

"There be more evil in this world than what can be accounted for in the hearts of men," Jeremy said with sadness. "Your Captain and ship, the Kellem, sails under a darkness. I seek to put an end to that darkness before she pulls the whole world asunder."

"Lies," Sam Brantley cried out. "The Captain is a good and God-fearing man."

"Quiet, you fool," ordered Henry Irons sternly. "Do not arouse these men before you are privy to the whole story."

"Man need not fear God, only the evil others do in His Name." Jeremy continued, "and your Captain may not know whom he serves. She is an old and very powerful Mermaid who has control of your ship and your Captain. Caused him to send innocent men to the locker and punish her daughter by breaking my neck. She will continue to inflict pain and suffering until her reign is ended."

"Aye, this be a story as old as the sea. Milady, you be a mermaid too? I tell you I would cry false, as my ignorant friend here does, if not for you two before me, true."

"What you heard is truth," Shera said, her voice like music on the wind to the men. "My mother will see every ship broken and all sailors on the bottom before her day is done."

"I have a plan," Jeremy told the trio, "being dead gives one a new perspective on life. A mermaid must return to the sea during the full moon or become human forever more. And no more powers will she possess. Truly spoken?"

"Yes, this be so," confirmed Shera.

"Then we must take captive the Kellem. Mr. Irons, can I trust you to be this ship's Boson."

"I would be privileged, Sir."

"Good. Then Mr. Brantley, you shall be the First Mate. And gentlemen, let us keep this amongst ourselves. It is bad enough that the men sail with a pirate's mark, let us not add the weight of mermaids and war to their duty load as well. Mr. Irons, I trust you know where the Kellem is heading?"

Shera returned to the Captain's Quarters as the men prepared to set sail.

Mr. Brantley whispered to Henry Irons, "this all seems like a bit of madness to me. Are you sure we can trust the Captain's orders?"

"Follow my orders when they seem just, for my judgment may be tainted by revenge," Jeremy responded, having overheard the query. "But trust hers at all time." He pointed to where Shera had disappeared. "Her heart has never wavered."

Shera plotted a course for the Islands, with a quick stop in Baltimore, as Jeremy needed to take care of the business of equipping the ship first. There, they traded eight of their twelve guns for four twenty-pounders and special exploding cannonballs. He mounted one on either side of the ship in the center, one in the bow, the other in the stern and called the new style cannons the Devastators, because one shot could blow a ship's hull apart. The lightweight cannonballs meant that they could be fired at a greater distance and still effectively sink the enemy before it had a chance to engage. Aided by the length and slender cannon barrel, the ball would be delivered with a great deal of speed and therefore force, guaranteed to penetrate any hull. He kept the four remaining six-pounder cannons on deck to use in close quarter combat when boarding would become necessary.

Trading the eight cannons for four also lightened the ship, making the Emerald Lady even faster under full sail, and speed was essential if they were to catch the Queen. They also had to be able to come upon a ship and be ready to fire from any angle.

"This is not what I thought we would do. I thought you agreed to capture my mother and take away her powers." Shera argued as the weapons were loaded and mounted within the decks. The aft Devastator below her nautilus.

"Those with power will not relinquish it without overwhelming force being brought to bear on them. All powerful people are the same; they only differ in your eye and tongue." He knew Rehema would not risk killing her daughter and ending her game so soon. She was more like a cat with a mouse. Trap it, beat it up a bit then let it run, only to pounce on it again. And as far as their personal battle was concerned, he was the mouse. But at their next encounter he would be ready. She was, after all, also flesh and blood.

Jeremy called First Officer Brantley to his quarters. "Mr. Brantley, we are going to need colors. Take this sketch and give it to the man with the steadiest hand."

Mr. Brantley looked at the drawing and then at the Captain questioningly. "Will not the men be put off by such a design?"

"It is a pirate's flag," Jeremy joked, "any design would be off-putting."

"But would not the traditional Skull and Bones be more appropriate? The men already ask questions. What with weapons meant to destroy rather than disable."

"I suppose, but we are not traditional pirates now, are we? And perhaps these colors will answer some of those questions for you."

They left port and headed for the Caribbean Seas, knowing that the Kellem patrolled the British islands looking for French or Spanish ships heading to the colonies to aid in the Revolution. The actions at Boston, the dumping of the tea, and the subsequent British crackdown had led to all-out war on land. Stopping supply ships from reaching the coast was the Kellem's main duty, along with protecting safe harbors for the British fleet.

The Emerald Lady, flying French colors, headed for the mainland. She was low in the water, cruising slowly, and was soon spotted by the Kellem, which began to close on her, coming within a mile. Captain Virgil Barnes ordered all hands-on deck. "To your battle stations men, let us send these French bollocks to a wet nesting."

Chapter 12
Tides of War

Jeremy ordered the French flag down from the Main mast and the hoisting of the Emerald Lady's new colors, which flapped tautly in the breeze. Its design, on the black of a pirate's insignia was that of a green mermaid with wild flaming red hair sitting on a crescent moon, her tail wrapped around it, and a cutlass held aloft in her right hand. He then ordered the ship to take a quarter turn towards the Kellem and to drop her sails to half-mast. The Emerald Lady began to slow to an almost stop, the men worked the bilge pump, and the ship, becoming lighter, rose in the water, ready for battle.

James L Hill

Jeremy called on Irons and Brantley, "you say your Captain is a good man, so here is his chance to prove it. Row over and tell him I wish for his presence aboard the Emerald Lady. We can avoid the cost of lives in a battle."

The men rowed across with two oarsmen and two gunners, climbed aboard their old ship and delivered the message.

Captain Barnes answered, "this is some sort of trickery, Mr. Simmons is dead. Unless the hangman poorly tied the knot. At any rate, I will not sully my rank by coming under a pirate's color. However, I am interested in what this pirate's aim is. I will meet him in longboats at half length, a single pistol man apiece. And Mr. Irons, it is a true shame to see your career end at the rope."

"Aye, my Captain," agreed Henry Irons, and then added his new-found wisdom, "but sometimes at the end of one's rope is the beginning of a new life."

As agreed upon, the two Captains were rowed out to a mid-way point between ships. Everyone was unarmed except one man with a pistol in each boat. He had one duty, at the first sign of trouble, kill the opposing Captain.

Captain Barnes remarked, "I would not have believed it, Mr. Simmons, but it is you! I don't know what bargain you have with the Devil, but I hope you paid in full before coming out here."

"It is you who serve the Devil," Jeremy traded jabs, "one of your men is not as he seems, in fact, she hides behind a false nature. You already killed one innocent crew, so before you commit more to their graves, I will have you strike your colors and turn your vessel and crew over to me."

"She! You think I sail with a sea-witch, as do you." The Captain looked for a sign from Jeremy but he remained stone-faced. "There has been talk of your ship, its Captain, and I think it may very well be true."

"Then if you believe all that you have heard, all the more reason to surrender your ship and save your men."

"And just like that," Captain Barnes blustered, "I give you the King's ship and men."

Jeremy eyed the Captain hard. "Those who will remain with you can board the longboats and be towed to safe waters."

"This is all very interesting, Mr. Simmons, but you are forgetting that I have you out-gunned twenty to six on either tack. What makes you think that standing and fighting will be different for you this time?"

"In Boston you gave me the courtesy of a warning shot across the bow," Jeremy's recusant voice turned ominous, "then, you hanged my men. I will let you return to your ship and I will return the courtesy. You shall have ten minutes to decide your fate and that of your crew."

"And you. Do not forget I put the noose to your neck also," Captain Barnes said as his oarsmen began to pull away.

Back onboard, Jeremy stood on the forecastle. Watching the Captain go to the helmsman, he commanded, "hoist the sails, and load the Fore Devastator, half powder and a short fuse."

The bow of his ship swung towards the Kellem and when reaching eleven o'clock, he yelled, "FIRE!"

The cannon belched flames, smoke, and thunder from a front hatch as it hurled a cannonball towards the other ship. The cloud trail abruptly erupted into a blaze and thunder rocked both craft. Fragments of red hot iron whizzed past the Captain's head and imbedded themselves in his ship. A couple of fragments ripped through the sails and started a fire but buckets of water quickly doused the flames.

Captain Barnes realized quickly that his ship was still out of range for even his biggest guns and that the Emerald Lady could and probably would blow it apart at any moment. Being a pragmatist, he ordered his colors to be taken down and told his men that those who wished to join him to get the longboats and prepare to abandon ship.

All officers and half the crew took to the longboats, Captain and followers shackled together. Heavy iron cuffs had been bolted onto their wrists, which in turn were chained to ankle bracelets with a long chain running through a ring between them, holding all men in the boats. And these, were coupled together one after another and then attached to the stern of the Emerald Lady. Jeremy sent four men up the Mizzen mast with four muskets each and ordered them to shoot anyone who attempted to escape.

Shahira was also aboard as one of the Kellem crew, in the holding cell with the other sailors who had refused to leave, hoping the Queen revealed her whereabouts, as she was certain Rehema had not had time to flee while so much had taken place. Moreover, the full moon would be in two nights. Rehema needed to return to the sea before then, or lose her mermaid powers. Something Shahira knew she would never do.

"Shahira cannot keep watch indefinitely," Shera complained, "she too must return to the water."

"I know, and she will be released before the time comes." Jeremy reassured her. "She is merely watching for Rehema's breakout."

"If she makes it to the water, she will not only retain her power but become stronger. I do not know if Shahira will be able to stop her."

"If she is in one of the longboats, we will shoot her before she can free herself, and if she is on board then there is no chance of her getting out."

Jeremy changed shooters at each ship's bell, and when the full moon arose, he doubled the men on the yardarms. He imagined that Rehema would choose to be among the men in the open boats, as it would give her easier access to the water. But when she tried, he would kill her.

He stood watch on the Quarterdeck, the full moon high in the night, and Shahira in the water. She swam beneath the Emerald Lady, watching the longboats with interest but so far nothing was out of the ordinary.

Then, suddenly, when the moon was about to set, a young sailor in the middle boat began to scream and flay his arms as he tried to jump. "Let me out of these chains, or I promise that I will kill all of you."

The boat swayed dangerously and Jeremy ordered the men to fire, but before a shot rang out the boat capsized and sank, taking eight men down with it.

Shahira raced as the other longboats began capsizing one by one and men awoke in terror. Reaching the middle boat, she searched for the man who had tried to escape, and placing a hand to his head, announced. *It's not her.*

Down in the holding cell of the Kellem, one small and rickets-stricken sailor who had been sitting on a bench a little away from the others, sprung to his feet, charged the wall with brute force, and broke several boards. A rather unnatural event for all present to witness, as not even the strongest of men would have attempted such a feat. It was suicidal. Water poured through, instantly creating an ever-expanding fissure on the side of the ship, and it began to flood. The crew panicked. Trapped below deck as the sea rushed in, Rehema transformed before the shocked sailors and smiled her wickedness broadly, reveling in their horror.

Shahira, she is aboard the Kellem, and is going to sink it too.

And I am sorry I cannot stop that. But I will try to catch her before she disappears.

The Kellem keeled over onto her side and within minutes disappeared under the waves. In the ensuing

169

pandemonium, Shahira darted back and forth, trying to rescue sailors if possible, as well as hoping to catch Rehema before she escaped. But she was too late for either. On reaching the holding cell under water, there were only dead sailors. The Queen was no longer onboard.

After the sinking of the Kellem, Aberash ordered all maidens to capture the Queen outright. None liked taking part in the affairs of men, but Rehema had left them no other option. Now, Aberash realized also that Rehema must have been meddling in the world of men for decades and probably had control over some very powerful people. The only question was, who, and from what nation.

Raakel, Shahira, and Shreya disguised themselves as figureheads on French Naval vessels, appearing to all as wooden carvings. They would control the ships' Captains, and in so doing, being able to avoid direct confrontation with the British. But it would only be a matter of time before Rehema's pot-stirring would force them to lead their ships into battle.

Across the ocean, Rehema had been fished out of the sea by the British frigate, The Horizon, which had been heading for the conflict in the Americas. Dressed as a junior officer from the Kellem, she was summarily brought before the Captain to give her account.

"The ship approached flying the French colors. We gave them a wide berth, a mile at the least. They becalmed our vessel by stealing our wind. Then they fired their gun. One shot broadside and the ship was lost."

"The name or markings of this ship, man," commanded Captain Maxwell Bell.

"A brigantine proper with seaweed green sails flying the pirate's mermaid flag; that is how you will know her. And her pirate Captain is Jeremy Simmons. He is well known in these waters."

"Aye," the Captain nodded. He was new to this part of the world, but he had heard some rumors already.

Which, Rehema had been only too eager to spread at ports, and on ships. Taking control of one man's mind then another, telling horrific tales of plunder and barbaric combat by the ruthless pirate Captain Simmons. She even told of a chest of gold, diamonds, rubies, and sapphires, and naturally, of colossal emeralds, his personal favorite.

"I heard he has an emerald onboard so large it takes a dozen men to lift it." He said.

"Aye, Captain, thus this name of his, The Emerald Lady," she fueled his imagination. "And his weapons can send a Man-of-war to the bottom before you can fire a single shot. Such guns can win battles."

The Captain ordered, "get this man some proper clothing and a meal, and a double ration of rum right away. You, return to the watch tonight. I mean to take down this pirate scum. Make sure these letters of charges are posted at every port."

The Horizon was a new type of warship. Smaller and narrower, which meant it was more maneuverable. She had one cannon deck with guns offset on either side so they had longer barrels and fired at a greater range. With three masts and a full square sail rigged, she could attack swiftly. And for that very purpose, The Horizon had been built to assail other ships and port cities, and been specifically sent to lay waste to the American colonies' newly formed navy, and to shut down their ports.

Rehema found it to be just the vessel she required to crush her sisters and daughters, and their siding with the French had been more than fortuitous; it was exactly as she had planned. The British and French had already gone through one costly war, so now, by drawing the colonies into the battle, their devastation would be complete. The colonies would be wiped out in this part of the world, the great navies would be sunk, and men would return to their own little territories once more, content to remain within their borders.

However, there was one glaring problem in the Queen's plan now, and not a small one at that, the Emerald Lady. Not only did she have to battle the Captain's will and that of her daughter's, but the power of her guns and swiftness were a genuine threat. She sat weighing her options and quickly realized that a battle on the open sea would probably cost her the Horizon, but if not, then it would indisputably be the destruction of the Emerald Lady, and possibly Shera's death. So no, because although she disliked the vessel greatly and wished it annihilated, she was also enjoying the game of cat and mouse immensely and wasn't about to let her daughter off that easily, or so soon.

Captain Bell got word that the Emerald Lady was sighted in the lower Chesapeake Bay. Retreating from the blockade of Philadelphia in the Delaware Bay, he headed south, planning to be at the mouth of the Chesapeake in two days and surprise Captain Simmons as he made for open waters. Rehema tried to convince the Captain that the reports were a trick to break the blockade.

"My good man, I have it on reliable loyalist sources that she is resupplying the Virginian colonies. This will be our best opportunity to send her and her Captain to the bottom."

"Of course, Captain." Rehema nodded. She knew some men were harder to persuade than others and the prize the Emerald Lady presented was impossible to pass up. Blind ambition and the thought of glory defeating the scourge of the western seas, though the reputation was a complete fabrication of Rehema's making, it had Captain Bell set on his course.

She waited until nightfall to dive overboard and entering the water without as much as a ripple, she transformed quickly, headed for the Chesapeake Bay, and found the Emerald Lady at anchor exactly as Captain Bell had said.

Helmsman, cut the anchor line.

The helmsman obeyed at once and the ship drifted down the Bay, and by the morning watch she was out to sea. Jeremy didn't have to wonder how; he could see

Rehema's handiwork, and sense her presence. By the noon bell a British schooner had been set ablaze off the coast of North Carolina, and fearing another trap, Jeremy made port in South Carolina. Striking the sails, he hoped to hide among the cargo ships.

Before the day was out, it was common knowledge that a survivor off the schooner had identified the Emerald Lady as the attacker and reported her heading to the southern coastal towns. He was also quick to add that several British Men-of-war were already on their way, led by the Horizon. Rather than chancing falling into Rehema's hands again, Jeremy set sail for the Caribbean Seas and the protection of the French territories.

North of Bermuda, in the early morning hours, the Emerald Lady was spotted by two English Men-of-war. They maneuvered to squeeze her behind them and opened fire. Musket balls and shrapnel peppered the decks, inflicting fatal wounds on all caught in its cloud. The Men-of-war had loaded their big guns with two or three loads of light armaments, determined not to sink her but to take the ship whole.

Jeremy also tried to avoid sinking the vessels, yet he knew that his crew could not withstand a second pass from the warships. Shera, terrified by the battle that raged around her, braced herself as she hid in the nautilus. Before their stern passed out of aim of his Devastators, Jeremy ordered the cannons to life, rocking the Emerald Lady violently from side to side from the repercussions. Unlike ordinary cannons mounted on wheel and set in tracks, the Devastators were fixed in place, all their fire power used to propel the cannonballs, which explained why each shot could pierce the thickest of hulls at close range.

The cannonballs slammed into the tail end of the ships below the Captains' quarters, creating small holes in their sides well above the water line. Seconds later, the quarterdecks erupted, the ships' rudders tore away, and flames and smoke raged from the rear, engulfing the sails. Within a minute, secondary explosions rang out. The men onboard, those not killed by flying debris within the craft, turned from fighting the Emerald Lady to fighting to save their ships and their own lives.

Lives have been claimed. Today, we have become the enemy.

Shera, we must fight to stay alive. Your Mother is the true enemy.

We are all the enemies of peace.

Jeremy understood her sadness, and brought her the critically wounded. Some she saved, others, and for her the number was too high, she released to the peaceful dream. Blood burnt and stained her skin, so he went into the sea with her that night, holding her for a time then floated alongside the ship in the calming waters.

She had finally seen the aftermath of battle. Previously, she had examined the sunken ships but never been part of or witnessed an actual clash. Was this truly the domain of men? Was her mother, right? Jeremy, as noble as he was, had taken pride in giving the order, and there had been a measure of glee as he watched the two ships limp away. Even the men who had come to her for peace relished in the victory of war.

There was singing and music aboard the Emerald Lady that night as they reveled in the events of the day. Shera moved among the men – a rare occurrence for her and them – dressing wounds and pouring rum and she was certain the liquid had a lot to do with the songs they shared. She knew it relieved the pain of missing limbs and damaged organs, but what brought them such joy?

It is the joy of still being alive. Jeremy consoled her.

The events of the day weighed heavier on her than on the men. Some were new to battle, and some had had their share already, but all knew what to expect. And having gone through it, they found living to be its own source of joy.

I have lived three hundred years and never experienced times like these. I have been among men for three and have been visited upon by more horrors than I care to know. I do not see how I can live out my seven hundred more like this.

I swear upon my grave that you will not.

The Emerald Lady had not been too badly damaged in the encounter, but her crew was less the wear in fighting strength and spirit. She made port in Jamaica, a British port and Jeremy had had another name plaque made and hung over her real name, it read The Sea Queen. He released the crew for further medical attention, only keeping a few healthy and able-bodied onboard to make repairs. It was a smart move; the one place the British navy would not be looking for him was at a British port.

The local governor was loyal to the Crown, but like most officials, he was more loyal to his purse. A hefty count of coinage and gems kept ships' names, of any sort, off the official registers.

Jeremy and Shera remained on board while the rest of the crew worked on repairs and quartered ashore. They went into town on occasion, but she soon grew pale and weak the further she travelled away from the water. She never made it more than a mile inland before collapsing and having to be carried back to the Emerald Lady. Proof that news of the Revolutionary War had not yet ended Rehema's reign.

Indeed, it grew stronger. For the Queen not only had the English navy firmly in hand with maidens serving on nearly every ship in the line but she also revived old alliances among the French, Spanish, and Portuguese, assuring dominance, and mayhem.

In the June of 1778, the Horizon pulled into the Port of St. George, Jamaica, with its very small docks in a closed and protected bay. It was not long before Rehema stood on the Emerald Lady's, or rather, the Sea Queen's deck.

At her orders, troops arrested Jeremy without delay and took him to the local prison.

Rehema went down to the Captain's quarters directly. *I never really liked this ship anyway. So, I will remove my name from her and find you a proper pirate crew to tend to your needs. And this time, I will make sure you never set eyes on your love again.* She told Shera.

Jeremy was led into the courtroom with shackled hands and feet. He stood passively, not listening to the long list of charges against him; instead, he searched the crowd, looking for the Queen. Surely, she would not miss this. He spotted her sitting in the front row with the governor, to whom he had paid good money to keep his secret, but clearly, she must have paid more.

He stared at her for a moment; she was just as he had seen her at his first trial years ago. *Oh, for a pistol and a shot!*

They would serve you well, but alas, I have other plans for you. And that cur of a daughter I spawned! Pay attention now, you are going to want to hear this.

The magistrate cleared his throat. "By order of His Majesty, for crimes on these high seas of piracy, and acts of war against the Crown, I hereby sentence you, Mr. Jeremy Simmons, Captain of the Emerald Lady..."

Yeah, I know, to be hung by the neck until dead. Didn't you at least tell them that sentence has no meaning anymore?

Listen!

"... To be put to death by beheading in the public square. Immediately, on this day, July 6th 1778 in the year of our Lord. And may God have mercy on your miserable... worthless... soul."

Jeremy leapt from the defendant's podium and onto the Sergeant at Arms, trying to wrestle the pistol from his belt, but there were too many hands dragging him away. Then he felt a sickening thud on the back of his head and his forehead bounced off the courtroom floorboards...

His eyes were blurry and pain emanated from both the front and back of his head. He could hear buzzing flies about dead meat, but it slowly turned to voices, then shouts, loud jeers, and finally insults.

As he struggled to focus his eyes it dawned on him that he was kneeling, his hands and feet still chained together, then fettered to the chopping block beneath his head. Flies crawled in front of his eyes and he smelled the rancid dry blood-soaked wood. The hot sun on his face was cooled for a moment by a shadow that stretched out in front of him. And at the end of what appeared to be a monster of a man was the distinct curvature of an axe.

Instinctively, he struggled against the chains then realizing the futility of his actions, relaxed. Taking a deep breath, he held it for a few seconds. *At least this will put an end to all this misery. And Shera, you will be free.*

Ha, ha, ha. Did I say this was the end?

He heard a sickening swish and thud then a gasp for air filled his ears. He rolled over, hit the ground, and found himself staring up at the man-monster holding the bloody axe.

Man-monster reached towards Jeremy's face.

He felt himself swinging through the air and for a split second saw his own body spurting blood and convulsing beside the chopping block. He registered the crowd cheering for a moment then fade to silence. Darkness was closing in on him fast, as if he were falling into a deep sleep. At least this time there was no pain.

The spectacle over, the crowd went about their daily routines, mending nets, selling fish, and drinking rum. The executioner unchained Jeremy from the block and was about to remove the manacles from his wrists and ankles when a female voice interrupted.

"No, leave those on," said Mrs. Cutter-Smythe, "and I will have his head in this box here."

"As you please, Madam," said the executioner and tossed the head into the small bejeweled chest at her feet.

"No need for uncouth treatment." She told him then kicked the chest's lid shut and locked it. "Take care, my good man."

The executioner dumped Jeremy's body into the long chest on a buckboard cart alongside the chopping block with likewise reverence as he had had for his head then slid two bars into the metal loops in the hood and body from opposite ends. In the center, he placed the shackles and bar together, locked the padlock, handed her the skull-headed key and remarked. "This is a lot to go through for one lousy pirate. Be ye afraid he will return to collect his due?"

Mrs. Cutter-Smythe placed the small chest on top of the ornate coffin, "I am sure he will try."

Discreetly, Mr. Irons and Mr. Brantley watched the proceedings, studying the stately woman who took the horse's reins and rode out of town in the buckboard cart with their Captain as its cargo. With nothing else to do or anywhere to go, they followed her on foot from a safe distance.

Shera curled up inside the nautilus, her eyes black. Tears burning down her cheeks, she chanted and sang a low wailing guttural sound. All across Jamaica a cold wind blew and everyone heard and felt its moan.

Port St. George returned to its riotous nature once the Royal Navy left. Boarding houses and ale inns were packed, the cane ships had sailed, and anyone who had been left behind was desperate to sign onto some kind of vessel.

Rehema entered one place and asked the proprietor to point out some men who were eager to sail. However, upon hearing the name Sea Queen, the man told her, "There be no pirates in my place. Nothing but honest seamen here, Milady."

Rehema tried another place and then another, each place louder, each place with men of lessening moral convictions. Then finally, she was at the Ball and Cock Inn. The men, in various stages of drunkenness cavorted with women in various stages of undress, who in turn, provided pleasurable services for coin and drink. Several men eyed her suspiciously.

She had stopped being discrete as to her business, so she announced loudly. "I am looking for a crew of twelve to twenty men willing to share the risk and rewards of a life aboard the Sea Queen."

Getting no immediate answer, she probed their minds for interested thoughts and found a group at the back of the bar. Making her way through the tables, she approached the eight men. "You look like an adventurous lot. What say you?"

A burly man stood up, towering over her, "You look like a proper bird, not the sort that be looking to go pirating."

"Call it what you like, are ye men interested?"

He continued. "Likewise, you can call her the Sea Queen or the Emerald Lady; she is still a pirate ship. Also haunted to boot. So, Milady, what else are you offering?" And without warning, he grabbed her and slammed her down hard onto the table. "Let's see what you really have to offer."

Rehema sprang up with a fist to his face. The three-hundred-pounder stumbled back, taking several tables out as he fell. The other men, momentarily amazed, grabbed hold of her and pulled her back down onto the table, ripping at her clothes, her blouse, skirt, petticoat, fighting each other as much as her. The tavern's crowd cheered wildly while others tried to force their way to her to get a turn, their minds too drenched in alcohol for her to reach. One stuck his hand under her skirt and she snapped her legs shut, crushing the bones, driving him to his knees, screaming in agony. Abruptly, her mind connected with one man, who was outside the tavern, his attention drawn by the sounds of mirth and mayhem. *Please, Sir, give aid.*

The thin Spaniard burst into the place and saw through the crowd the woman under siege. His yells for all to halt were drowned out in the bedlam and fell on deaf ears. Quickly digging a fumbling hand into his pocket, he pulled out a small pistol nervously, cocked it, and fired it above his head. There was instant silence in the tavern, all faces turned towards the door, towards the thin and frail Spanish missionary standing beneath a cloud of gun smoke. "I think you lot should unhand that woman."

The burly man who had started the riot pushed to the front and center of the crowd, "This be no place for a man of God, preacher. You fired your one shot; now go, before you need someone to pray for you."

"The thing about prayer, Sir, is this. God always provides to those in need." The missionary pulled another much larger pistol from his waist sash and aimed it at the large man's head. "And the woman is coming with me. Unless you would like to take the matter up with The Almighty... personally."

Rehema jumped to her feet and the men cleared a path. Pulling her blouse together, she took her time straightening the rest of her clothes. Walking purposely to the preacher, she turned back to the burly man, "I have found my Bosun. So, you, and as many as these bilge rats as you can bring be ready to sail at dawn's light."

"You can't trust these men, Madam," objected the missionary, "surely there must be others that would make a more capable crew."

"Not for what I need them to do," Rehema took the missionary by the arm. "And you are right, I can't trust them. But I can trust their Captain."

"Madam, surely you jest, I am no ship's Captain. I am here, by order of his Holiness, to bring God to the heathen savages."

"The savages have their own God. And you will find no greater gathering of heathens than aboard the Emerald Lady come dawn." Rehema began leading him to the docks. "Come, let me show you why I will trust no other to Captain her."

Rehema led the missionary into the Captain's quarters, going through the office and into the bedroom. She opened the door at the back and revealed the glowing emerald nautilus in the darkened room. Unsurprisingly, he was instantly awed by the jewel's beauty, its carvings and inlaid gems projecting an astonishing light show in the chamber. But even as he was staring at its splendor, he was taken aback to registered movement within the enormous stone.

Come forth and meet your new master. Rehema commanded then turned to the missionary. "Those men's job will be to hunt and kill French sailors. Don't worry, there are Letters of Engagement from the British Crown giving rights to take Men-of-war and Merchant vessels to divide the spoil among the crew and His Majesty equally, one half for the ship and the other for the Crown." Placing a hand on the nautilus and with the slightest of efforts, she turned it on its side.

A flood of seawater rushed out, carrying Shera to the man's presence. The young woman curled up, trying to cover as much of her naked body as was possible.

Rehema grabbed her daughter by the hair and lifted her to her feet like a ragdoll, blatantly exposing her to the missionary.

Shera's thick flowing locks had thinned, shortened, and its scarlet beauty marginally concealed her breasts, merely reaching her navel. She was pale, almost bleach white, thin, and frail, but still a beautiful being by any means. Shaking from both fear and anger, she crossed her hands in front of her body, bowed her head, and fixed her gaze on her feet.

"Captain Macario Santiarra, this is the jewel you will guard with your life."

"By all that is Holy, Woman, what in Satan's name do you condemn me to?" The missionary was appalled by what was before him but could not look away.

You see, my daughter, I am not so bad. I sent your lover to the darkness once again, but I brought you this willow of a man. And even through his shame and disgust

185

you can still feel his desire and lust. Rehema turned the nautilus the right way up again, "now, let us get you properly attired, before you corrupt the good preacher entirely."

Rehema directed Santiarra to take the gold mail tunic that lay on the floor and to clothe Shera in it. It was a simple thing that went over her head, down to her feet, and an elaborate chain kept it locked around her waist. Then she instructed him to place her back in the nautilus, which had darkened and no longer displayed the enchanted symbols and colors. "I will leave you for a moment. The two of you may want to get to know each other."

"Milady, please, tell me what witchery has befallen you, and now ensnares me as well!"

Watching her mother retreat, Shera sank to the bottom of the nautilus, out of sight, and without a word.

Rehema returned within minutes, soaking wet, and carrying a full water-barrel on a shoulder. She put it down with the boom of a cannon shot, startling the missionary. In the other hand, she held three rum bottles by their neck, which she proceeded to crack at once over the edge into the barrel and let the contents and the bottles themselves fall in. Looking around the cabin, she found a tin drinking cup, scooped half a measure of the rum and seawater blend and carelessly tossed it into the nautilus.

Santiarra heard a faint sizzle from the shell. "Should I feed her?"

"You give her that much rations daily, no more, and she will guarantee your victory in battle. Never let the men

186

gaze on her, as you now know the effects. Feed her what you will, if she will eat, that is entirely up to you, but she is a pelagic being and exists on seawater," Rehema started to leave the cabin. "You will know your headings when the morning comes."

Next morning, the men from the Ball and Cock arrived at the dock. There were twenty-three and one boy, led by the big burly man Byron – but anyone who wished to live called him Bart – and the man with the broken hand wrapped in splints. "Boatswain Bart McCoulland, requesting to come aboard."

"Welcome aboard, sign the ship's registry, or make your mark," said Macario Santiarra. "Stow your gear below."

As the teenage boy went to write his name, the Captain grabbed his hand. "I don't think this be a voyage for one your age. What is your name, boy?"

Bart, who took up a position alongside the Captain to watch the men sign in answered, "don't know his proper name but he be called Jack Quick. Meself and mates fished him from the ocean some years ago, so he has been with us ever since. He don't talk much, don't eat much either, but he is as natural as a gull in the riggings. Oh, and he be sailing with us."

Macario was still afraid of the men, and they in turn were afraid of who had hired him, so everyone onboard thought it best to do what was expected of them. They dropped the Sea Queen plaque into the water and raised the sails once again as the Emerald Lady, heading out to sea on an easterly course. "Our first mark is a Jamaican sloop, France's Silent Fortune. She is leaving out of Hispaniola laden with treasures," announced Captain Santiarra.

As the Emerald Lady jumped into the wind, a strange calm overtook Jack Quick. Scampering up the chains to the Fore Top to look out for rocks and reefs, he felt as if he knew the ship, as if he were finally home.

Chapter 13
Gold, Lust, and Rum

As the sun passed over the yardarm, Bosun Bart piped the men to the line for their afternoon ration of grog and hardtack. Each man dipped his tin and filled it to the brim. Bart swung the cat-o'-nine-tails from his right wrist, "move smartly men and get back on station." The whip, as much as his stern warning, deterred any from double dipping. And as usual, Jack was last in line at the water barrel.

"How many years have ye now, boy?" Bart asked in a fatherly tone before Jack dipped his cup.

"As best as I can figure, I be sixteen years come my birthday," Jack told him.

"On what day were ye birthed, boy?"

"Now, that be the thing, Mr. Bart. I've been so long from me mother, I cannot rightly recall," Jack's voice turned sour.

"Then I say today be as good a day as any to celebrate your birth boy, take a full dip."

"Hoorah!" Cheered the men around the barrel as they parted into two rows.

As Jack started to take a step through the line, Bart swung the whip before him. "Ye be wanting to drink that down first, laddie."

Jack downed the cup of grog then he walked between the two rows of men, and was punched and jostled until he reached the tray of hardtack. Not once had he come off his feet. Another cheer went up among the men. Then he took his usual place at the foot of the Foremast and began to chew the tough bread. The men paraded past him adding a few drops of grog to his cup for him to moisten his bread.

Bart sat next to the boy, "Enjoy this day, Jack. For tomorrow you may have to kill a man from the Foretop. I need your aim true because every missed shot does not save a life, it costs another man his. Maybe even your own."

"Mr. Bart, what are we truly?" the boy asked. "Some of the men say we be Pirates. Some say we are Privateers."

"Don't trouble yourself with it. That distinction lies on which side of the gold you are on, the ones who we are stealing it from or the ones who we are stealing it for. The only thing I tell you here is, don't die for the gold. I will

190

make sure you have plenty of rifle and dry powder up top. And keep in mind; never fire your last shot before reloading another. Eat up and get back up there. Remember, a sloop is low on the water and will disappear in the waves. So, keep a sharp eye."

Bart often told Jack that the sea decided a man's fate; that he rode on the tides and was blown by the wind to wherever it wished him to be. They had fished Jack out of the sea as fishermen then before they could get him home, had been drafted into the Continental Navy as raiders. Bart, his men, and his ship had been pressed into service by the British Royal Navy to fight against his former allies. And now, this, the crew of a cursed ship.

"Aye. Aye. Mr. Bart. I will not let you down." Jack watched as the old man lashed a deckhand for no apparent reason as he passed him by.

When was his birthday? His mother would know. Strange that he would be thinking of her now. It was now four years, since he had gone into the ocean after the wreck of the Rummy Gale, and he still recalled vividly the red of her hair in the sunshine. But especially the smell of strawberry tarts she baked for him. Odd how he recalled every detail of his last birthday before his father took ill, before he had been caught in the grip of the fever and poured out his life onto the bed sheets. He had just turned twelve. His father gave him his old hunting musket as a present, which he never got to fire. He could remember everything, except the date.

Thomas Bushell, the man whose hand had been crushed and needed the Captain to cut it off a week into the voyage, was about to ring the ship's bell for the watch when Jack heard a sound.

'Bing… Bing…'

He called down to the Bosun, "Mr. Bart, I hear a ship's bell."

"How many, boy?"

"Two."

'Bing… Bing…'

"Just there, two more," Jack yelled.

But Bart had heard them as well. "Go alert the Captain, Mr. Bush-Grabber," that had become the man's nickname after losing his hand between a woman's legs. "Keep a sharp eye for that ship, boy."

"Aye… Aye, Mr. Bart." Jack pulled his spyglass from his pocket and scanned the horizon.

Bart ordered half a dozen men up the Main Mast, one to aid in looking for Silent Fortune, and five to quickly set the Main Sails.

The Captain joined Bart on the Forecastle and queried, "You have a sighting?"

"No. The boy heard four bells of the First Dog Watch, so the ship can't be too far ahead."

"What is your plan of action?" asked the Captain.

"Four bells," Bart said without a thought of who was in charge, "it will be dark soon. If we catch a sighting, we come to full sail and close in the darkness. If we don't get a sighting, we stay at half sails so as not to pass her in the night. Either way, no lanterns tonight. And no bells."

When night came, the sails were reefed and the men aloft were put on watch. It was midnight before Jack spotted a single light bobbing off the port bow. He alerted the Captain and the Bosun below immediately. They adjusted their course but left the sails as they were. The Silent Fortune was indeed heavy in the water and the Emerald Lady was gaining on her at half sail. They would be upon her before dawn.

Before first light, the men could hear the waves slapping the hull of the boat ahead of them but had seen no other lights that night. The Bosun figured the night watch had lit his pipe. His comfort would probably cost all his fellow sailors their lives.

With the sunrise, they saw the sloop coasting ahead at full sail. "Should we go to full sails now and come up on them broadside?" asked Captain Santiarra.

The Emerald Lady was half a mile to the starboard of the Silent Fortune. "No Sir, we are just about where we need to be. We will swing behind them and hit her with our forward gun. We take out their rudder first then we can pound them from any angle we want. I will make a proper pirate out of you yet, preacher."

"Wait, don't start the battle yet, I almost forgot the most important weapon we carry." The Captain ran down the stairs and across the weather deck into his quarters, grabbed a black sack and busted into the inner chamber. "Come sea-witch, it is time for your magic."

Shera was curled up at the bottom of the nautilus, a few inches of rum and seawater wetting her hip. Captain Santiarra grabbed her arms and pulled her from the tub, struggled to get her in the sack, and when she was finally secured, he hefted her onto his shoulder. He ran down the gun deck and the men stared at him and the obvious body he carried. Then he went through a small door to the bow bulkhead and down three steps, opened a double wooden door, placed Shera inside the figurehead, and pulled the sack off her, "You may want to see this."

He slammed and padlocked the double doors, composed himself and walked up the three steps again.

The men were standing and staring into the dark hole in the bulkhead.

Captain Santiarra banged the door shut and padlocked it as well. "What the hell are ye all looking at?" he yelled, "back to your stations."

There was rumbling among the men and as Santiarra left the gun deck, he heard one say, "The madness on this ship has reached a new height."

Unperturbed, he returned to the Bosun's side, "you may fire when ready, Mr. Bart."

They were five hundred yards dead aft of the Silent Fortune and had not been detected. Bart gave half a thought to just sliding up alongside of her and demanding a surrender. Then he gave the order, "bow gunner fire!"

The gunner touched the lit wick to the gun's primer; it fizzled for a second, just long enough for the gunnery crew to cover their ears. The cannon roared like a dragon from hell and Shera screamed with the pain. Smoke clouded her vision as she tried to peer through the holes in the figurehead. The ship's bow lifted and dropped hard on the ocean and jets of seawater sprayed through the cracks and carvings into the figurehead and the sudden life-giving water quickly washed away the grog's cloudiness she had been exposed to. She felt as if she had awakened from a nightmare, awaking just in time to see the back-end of the sloop explode. She had awakened from one nightmare and gone straight into another.

The Bosun and the Captain watched the cannonball crash through the back of the vessel. Seconds later, they stared in amazement as the back of the Silent Fortune was torn apart, the ship's wheel thrown high in the air, hitting the water with a violent splash ahead of them.

"Well, I guess we disabled their ship." Said Santiarra.

"Are you mad, man," yelled the Bosun, "one shot and we nearly sent her straight to the bottom."

Mr. Santiarra, fire again.

"Mr. Bart, pull alongside and we will hit her with a broadside," ordered Captain Santiarra.

"Did you hear me, Mr. Santiarra," the Bosun said, "one more shot from these guns and that ship is going down. And her treasure with her."

I said I want that ship. Take her at the bow. Fire on it now.

"That is Captain Santiarra, and I said full sails." The missionary suddenly roared like the cannon. "We will give her one pass at the bow then we can board her."

Bart ordered full sail and started the pass, also ordering the port deck cannon ready for firing. As they passed, the two top carronades sent forth a barrage of death and Bart gave the order to begin the boarding. The Silent Fortune was taking on water from the rear and listing badly. They got lines on the ship and tied her up while the boarding party raided the holds.

Half the inside decks were splintered and destroyed, two of the holds flooded and unreachable. They emptied the stores quickly then returned to their ship and the Bosun ordered them to take the medium-sized cannons as well. After the looting, he allowed the crew to board the longboat and row away but any critically injured man was to be left aboard to go down with the ship.

Shreya had found her way into the figurehead of Neptune on the bow of the Silent Fortune, the statue was big and bulky but still gave her little room as she infused her body with that of the wood. Her spirit was in touch with every man onboard and with the maidens as well. It was overwhelming being linked to a hundred and sixty-four men, her sisters, and maintain a semi-solid form simultaneously. She soon found it necessary, although less efficient, to only link with key people aboard the Silent Fortune. And she stayed constantly vigilant as she could feel the Queen's presence nearby.

She found the night easier, as most of the men were asleep and only a few active thoughts filtered through the wood. Shreya felt the night helmsman at the wheel; he was bored and longing for home and wife. He had been hearing stories for months of the war with the colonists and how tensions were once again high between George and Phillip. The Brits were in need of monies, and a cargo of cane, tobacco, and gold would be a temptation, he imagined.

Until they got out of the Island waters, the ship operated under reduced standards, such as the ringing of the ship's bell only every sixth hour, no lanterns on night watches, and four men aloft in the crow's nest at all times. After the sounding of the midnight bell, all was quiet aboard, and the helmsman decided that it was a good time for a pipe. He lit it up and enjoyed it sweet flavor.

Shreya felt danger in the darkness instantly. She had been concerned because she had lost contact with Shera, through Jeremy, a week previously, so she was certain what it meant, as she felt nothing from him and when she set her mind to his, there was only blackness. She alerted the Captain. *Look alive my Captain, trouble lurks.*

The Captain took a turn on the weather deck, checked the canvas on the guns and slid his hand under a couple to feel for moisture on the fuses. If battle was upon them, he would not lose to a damp wick. Coming to the helmsman, he smelt the smoke in the air about him, "Sir, having a smoke while on duty? Consider yourself on report and half rations for the week."

"Aye, Sir," responded the helmsman.

"Mind you, sir, the sea has long eyes, especially at night."

"Aye, Sir. I beg the Captain pardon."

"There be no pardons," replied the Captain, "but no lashes either. These are troubled waters, so keep that pipe in its pouch until the proper time." Then he returned to his cabin, paused for a moment, and looked back off the quarter deck.

"Sails aft the starboard," called a lookout from the Main Crow's Nest at first light then pulled out his spyglass and took a longer look. "A green sailed brigantine, I make it to be the Emerald Lady."

Shreya felt nothing but dread and death about the ship, could not feel Jeremy at all, and only a hazy confusion when she tried to fix her mind on Shera. Something was terribly wrong aboard that vessel. *Captain, trust no friend or foe.*

The Captain ordered all hands-on deck and watched the Emerald Lady with interest. She had been an ally of the Colonies, but his interest turned to concern as she altered course to move directly behind him. He ordered the quarter deck guns to the ready. His ship was heavy and could not out-run the old brigantine but he could out-maneuver her if a fight was what she was after. His aft guns would slow her down until he could get a more favorable position.

He saw the British Jack take its position below the Mermaid insignia of the Emerald Lady, knowing she had been turned. Fire and smoke obscured her bow and seconds later his ship was jolted by a cannonball through the stern.

The iron ball bounced along the berth deck below them, beating like a drum, then crashed into the Mizzen Mast, and rolled backwards against the port side, smoking ominously. The Captain was about to return fire but never got the chance to give the order. The cannonball exploded.

On the quarter decks, wooden spearheads impaled the sailors, who were thrown from the ship without warning, many killed instantly, including the Captain. A flaming cloud raced forward through the ship setting ablaze everything in its path and crushed it all against the bow. The Silent Fortune's stern was pushed five feet below the waterline then recoiled back twice as high. All men onboard bounced like puppets on the fractured deck, a gaping hole appeared where the Captain's quarters should have been, and out of the scar, flames and smoke billowed.

Both Shreya and the Silent Fortune were critically wounded. Crimson flowed freely along decks, the wail of the injured was horrifying, and from the figurehead, rivulets of blood gushed into the sea.

The Emerald Lady came alongside and a second blast shook the ship. Grappling hooks and lines bound the Silent Fortune and kept the vessel momentarily afloat while the pirates raided her. Most of her crew was injured or dead, many already floating in the water. Half an hour after the first shot had been fired, lines were cut and the Silent Fortune was allowed to go to its final resting place.

Once on the bottom, Shreya freed herself from the vessel and lay down in the silt as the other bodies touched down gently around her, forming the Silent Fortune Graveyard. A hundred and seventeen bodies and souls were laid to rest that day. All maidens felt the loss of one of their own, and also felt the sorrow in the human world. When one man dies, all men feel it, even if they no longer recognize the feeling.

Only Rehema took joy in the scene then swam away looking for the next traitor and wasted no time in laying blame for Shreya's death on those she called Conspirators. She let it become known that the sisters had carved an emerald nautilus, which she professed gave Shera and Jeremy control over men. *These Conspirators, maiden and men alike, are moving to destroy Usea Maya and end my reign. I can no longer feel the man, Jeremy. And Shera's thoughts are all a mystery to me.*

I cannot either.

There is nothing save blackness where those two are involved.

Tell us what we must do.

You must find the Conspirators and bring them before me, even if that means sinking every ship man has on the seas.

Aberash grasped the seriousness of the situation all too quickly; Rehema has just gotten what she wanted. *My sisters, in our attempt to stop her, we handed the Queen exactly what she needed, an ultimate weapon to be used against both us and mankind. We must find the Emerald Lady and send her back to the bottom. We will try to save Shera at all costs, but I fear she may already be lost to us. I feel only sorrow and torment within her soul, and her mind is in a tempest.*

The Captain called all men to toe the line and the ship's crew responded by lining up on the weather deck, jubilant and willing to follow their leader. Santiarra ran below, needing to put his secret weapon back in her place. Unlocking the doors to the figurehead, he was met with a radiant Shera. The ocean spray had obviously done her good and he could not hold his desires as he turned her around to him. The golden mail dress kept her in place but she pushed him back and across the deck with one hand.

"Ah, so you come to life my little fish," he said as he wiped seawater from her face with his hand. "What a strange creature you be."

Forcing himself against her, he kissed her then taking his hand, squeezed her jaw, forced her mouth open, and dropped fervent kisses on her. She resisted. His left hand fumbled beneath her dress, but the golden chains were weighty. There was a bridge that ran from front to back connecting the panels between her legs and he could not get the access he desired.

Shera stopped resisting, instead, she held his face, her fingers stroking his temples gently. *Remove the belt. Lift my dress. Take what you desire.*

If you do, she will rip you in half, preacher. Dry her and take her to her cell. Give her a tight ration to calm her spirit, you fool.

Santiarra threw the sack over Shera and used it to rub her down. Then still dizzy with excitement, he lifted her into his arms and carried her to his quarters. He hesitated before the bed but a burning sensation pushed him into the inner sanctum. Gently slipping her into the nautilus, he pulled the sack from her head. She retreated from view quickly, dropping into the mucky water at the bottom. Grabbing the tin cup, he filled it with rum and drank it straight down then he poured another and slowly emptied it into the nautilus. "What a strange creature you are."

The Captain stumbled from the room, closed and locked the door. Turning, he was startled by Jack Quick standing at attention outside his door. "What do you want, boy? Why are you not standing in the line?"

"Mr. Bart sends me, Sir. Says the men grow impatient. He wants me to report, if the Captain is feeling fit."

"How long have you been there, boy?" Santiarra was becoming suspicious.

"I was just about to knock when you made your presence known, Sir."

"Tell Mr. Bart he may release the men to general quarters." He sat heavily at his desk. "Tell him also to bring me a manifest of all that was recovered from the Silent Fortune. And to make it smartly, no man is to receive a share before his Captain."

Jack started up the stairs to the weather deck but inexplicably, the same curious calm from before overcame him, pulling him towards the Captain's chambers. For a moment, an inner struggle filled him about which direction to take, but finally, the feeling passed and he went to deliver the message.

Rehema leapt from the water and landed softer than a kitten on the quarter deck. The helmsman slumped over the wheel and the night watchman slipped down and fell asleep in the Main Mast perch. She walked into the Captain's quarters.

Santiarra, immediately awakened from a deep sleep, blustered. "I did not touch her. Just did as you told me."

Is this what you desire?

Santiarra watched the naked woman, who was in a word, beautiful, then she became younger and more radiant, the lines on her face softened and disappeared. Her muscle tone strengthened and her complexion irradiated. Going from a fifty-year-old woman to a rosy-cheeked milkmaid of sixteen. Walking over to the bed, she climbed onto the missionary and smothered him in worldly delights he had never known.

At sunrise, Captain Santiarra joined Bart on the Forecastle. "Bring the ship about, Mr. Bart. We have a new target and a new heading. We head northwest in pursuit of the Grand Serpent."

"Aye, aye. Captain." The Bosun stood firm.

"Is there something on your mind, Mr. Bart?"

"Aye, Sir. Let me say, you have better color today. I thought once the blood fever left you yesterday— well, you were not quite all together, you know, being a preacher and all. Are you still a preacher? In the business of saving souls, or are you not?"

"Aye. That I am," Santiarra responded thoughtfully. "There be a great evil afloat here. And it seems God has set my course so that I may rid the world of it."

"Ah, that brings me to my second concern," announced Bart. "The cannonballs we carry are of an unsavory sort. Hollowed out and filled with powder. If Captain Jeremy Simmons was a pirate as charged, he was a very bad one. Such ordinance can only serve one purpose, to destroy a ship whole and entirely. He left his crew no chance to plunder her."

"So, what concern of this be mine, or yours, for what matters?"

"Sir, we be in the business of plundering and retrieving riches for the crew, and of course, the Crown. Let me give you an insight into the men of your crew. Their first loyalty is to the ship for it is their home and sanctuary. Their second loyalty lies with their brethren whom they expect to live and die with. The last and least of their support is to their captain, for he can be replaced when his orders run contrary to the first two interests. These ordinances be such a danger, a single stray musket ball will send us all face to face with our Creator. I say we stow them well below in the hold. Only bring them up for defensive purposes."

The Captain studied him for a moment then nodded in agreement, adding, "you can keep a round for each gun at the ready for our next encounter. The Grand Serpent is a ship of the line and she will be carrying no treasures. Only the souls God wants collected. For this purpose, she strengthens me in my resolve."

"She? Sir? Do you still serve the same Lord?"

"She? No! What, are you mad?" The missionary became flustered. "Everyone knows God is male. Set the course Bosun."

Bart turned and walked the deck swinging his cat-o'-nine-tails as he barked orders. Jack, sitting on the lowest yardarm, had heard the conversation and thought it rather peculiar. He too had noticed the change in the Captain and he knew it had to do with something in his private chambers. Perhaps the Captain would need cleaning in there, or he could steal a look while he was otherwise engaged. He would keep vigilant for an opportunity. Just as he was about to turn back to his duty as lookout, he heard. *The quarter deck at midnight.*

Jack snuck onto the quarter deck by climbing down a rope from the gaff sail.

 The helmsman turned for a second, as he was sure he had heard something land behind him, but nothing. Then peering through the skylight, he only saw the Captain in his bed.

 Jack crawled around the deck and found a crack to peek through and instantly saw the giant green nautilus. Something flashed within and he jumped up startled, "Mermaid!"

 Shhh. I need your help, Jack.

 "What... Hey, boy, what are ye doing there?" asked Bush-Grabber.

 "Nothing, sir. Can't sleep."

 "Well, do your ghost-walking somewhere else. Before I dangle ye from me hook."

 "Yes sir," Jack said and headed back towards the crew quarters. Back in his bunk, he began to put things together. The Emerald Lady, the green mermaid on their insignia, the huge nautilus in the Captain's quarters. They had a mermaid trapped aboard.

Yes. That's right. And only you can help me. You can save me.

"Tell me how," he whispered.

I need seawater, lots of seawater. And for you to remove my chains.

"Aye. I promise I will help you."

The Emerald Lady had been ambushed by the man-of-war named the Grand Serpent off the coast of New Jersey, and was now hiding in the marshes near Toms River awaiting the opportunity to strike back. She sailed out near dusk to start the delicate maneuvers that would allow her to bombard the ship, while the Grand Serpent was swinging out to sea to cut off her escape. She lobbed mortar shells, pushing the Lady closer to shore.

The Grand Serpent's plan was to run her aground and then take her apart piece by piece. And things were going as planned when the Captain of the Emerald Lady seemed to make a desperate move. He turned perpendicular to the shoreline, heading straight at the Serpent. The Serpent's Captain fired his port guns and all but two of the twenty-one cannonballs fell short in the water. A twelve-pound shot bounced down the deck, hammering three crewmen along the way, breaking deck planks and bones.

The second shot, balls and chain, whistled through the air. It slammed into the Foremast, shaking it from top to bottom. Jack was tossed from his perch, but luckily, was caught by the Forestay Sail. But he was not so lucky when he landed on the Forecastle, instantly breaking his arm and hitting his head on the deck. He was taken below deck to his bunk amid musket balls and cannon fire.

Shera heard Jack calling out to her. "You must abandon ship. They are going to sink the Emerald Lady." It might have been the boy's voice, but it was Raakel's words she heard.

"Keep your distance, our guns are ship killers, our cannonballs explosive," Shera warned from her cage in the figurehead, as she could see Raakel in the figurehead of the Grand Serpent. Then she yelled to Jack. "Take cover!"

Captain Santiarra shouted, "Forward gunner fire!"

Shera strained and drowned out the orders.

The Bosun bellowed, "Fire, you worthless dogs."

She could not affect the Bosun's command and the gun fired its deadly projectile at the Grand Serpent.

Three seconds later, Raakel caused the starboard gunners to fire their cannons in unison.

Their Captain yelled, "Stand steady men!"

The retort of cannon fire drove the vessel over and down and The Lady's cannonball flew over the deck and burst through the starboard railing, landing in the water, exploding where it did no damage.

Captain Santiarra ordered the sixty-eight-pounder carronades to fire as he swung back the Lady with the wind then he called for the starboard Devastator to fire and its cannonball struck its mark. It exploded on the upper gun deck, crippling the ship's port guns. Captain Santiarra was at full sail running south from the man-of-war, knowing that he was out-gunned and trapped against the shoreline, and it would only be a matter of time before the battle took its toll.

The Grand Serpent took a port tack to give chase. The vessel turned slower than the Emerald Lady and she put distance between them. Sailing against the wind also gave the smaller ship the advantage, so she managed pull away with only minor damages and three lost crewmen. But escape was not what was on Captain Santiarra's mind or the crew of the Emerald Lady.

In the dead of night, the Emerald Lady passed the Serpent on her crippled port side and managed to get off three shots with her Devastator. The Grand Serpent got off a round with the smaller deck guns but not enough to take down the Emerald Lady before she was burning, capsized, and gone.

Fortunately, Raakel had managed to dive back into the sea before the second encounter, and unseen, she jumped onto the Emerald Lady's figurehead and gazed into her sister's eyes. "We can reach you through the boy now and we are going to free you, but beware, everyone is out to sink this ship."

"Where is Jeremy? You have to find him, as I cannot reach him at all."

"There is nothing. We do not know what the Queen has done or where she has him." Raakel admitted.

"Break this cage and I will help you find him."

"If only I could," Raakel lamented, "that is gold you are wearing, I will not be able to carry you as it is too heavy, and you will drown. You know this. Use the boy, get him to free you from this chaining. And we will rescue you."

The celebration of the battles was more than Shera could take. The drunkenness and reveling in the bloodshed was driving her mad. She could hear them retelling how they had killed and when. But the boy was still unconscious, which caused her more concern. She heard voices through the wooden door.

"Captain, how is the boy?"

"Mr. Bart, I set his arm. His head took a bad knock but does not appear to have broken the bone. I believe he will recover in a few days, if God is with him."

"Captain, may I ask a favor of you?" Bart asked humbly, "I want to put the boy ashore in Virginia. He does not need this life."

"It may not be safe," the Captain said, "we will have to find a port held by the British."

Shera's spirits sunk even lower and she slammed a fist against the nautilus.

The Bosun's attention was drawn to the sound and he looked at the Captain, who avoided his gaze and question. Then he ordered the Bosun to unlock the rum barrel and let each man drink his fill. The Bosun left happy but confused. The Captain's secret weapon worked even when they were out-gunned. But for how long and at what cost?

Santiarra had once been a man of God, but now he was only interested in killing, leading these men on a dark and deadly course that could only end at the bottom of the sea. After each encounter, he returned Shera to the nautilus and doused her liberally with rum then turned the bottle on himself, drinking until he could feel no more. He knew he was out of control. The once bright eyes and proud savior of a women in distress was now only a shadow. His mind and body desired the green-eyed goddess trapped in his chambers, but he was at the command of Rehema and she would never let him be satisfied. He hated Shera. He hated Rehema. He hated all mankind. Most of all, he hated himself.

Jack's arm healed faster than his head, remaining unconscious for months. Partially from his injuries and mostly by Shera constantly lolling him to sleep. She knew this boy; he was the boy of Jeremy's rescue. And during that rescue, he had bonded with her. Now, she planned to keep him onboard by keeping him asleep. And as he slept he dreamt of his red-haired mother. Her hair flowing wild, caressing him, enveloping him, rocking him in a mother's loving embrace.

The Captain decided to retreat from the coast for the winter, heading for Island waters once more. But this time, he chose the twin Islands of the Caymans, a pirate's refuge. No naval vessel, British, French, or Spanish would enter those ports.

Shera's mind was filled with lurid dreams from the drunken crew. The only escape she had was with Jack in his dreams, who finally awoke after six months, weak and scrawny. The Bosun was still intent on sending him home; as the fall has left his eyesight blurred, he was of little use as a lookout now. He reassigned the boy to kitchen duties and scrubbing the decks. Jack enjoyed the work as he got to peek through the cracks in the quarter deck at Shera.

I am so weak. I need seawater.

Jack lowered his wash-bucket on a rope and pulled up a full load. As he washed the deck, he poured the water over the crack. Some managed to trickle into the nautilus, but not much. But it was enough to clear Shera's head of rum, and quell the voices of the drunken sailors.

At night, when all the men were asleep, Jack would sneak up to the quarter deck and lay there so he could be close to Shera. He had also started using his knife to widen the crack so he could get a better look at her. She was the most beautiful woman he had ever seen, even outshining the golden dress she wore. And when he swabbed the deck, a larger amount of seawater bathed her. The daily dose of rum had little effect on her now, thanks to Jack.

Jack, when the Captain goes ashore, I need you to free me from these golden chains.

I will, my love.

His thoughts disturbed her, she had not intended for Jack to regard her in this manner. But the hauling of water had built up his body and the passage of time had turned the boy into a man. He was now eighteen and the sight of her had the same effect on him as on the Captain. There was much confusion in Jack's mind. And Shera could feel the dark thoughts he had towards the Captain.

Santiarra was also growing suspicious. One day, while pouring the half cup of grog into the nautilus as was his custom, he peered inside to admire his prisoner. He stared, surprised, the water line had risen higher than half a cup a day would provide, she was in fact, waist deep. Shera glared at him and his mind caught fire, throwing himself against the wall to escape her view. Registering a single shaft of light from the deck above to the nautilus opening, he saw water trickling into the tub from the crack above.

Santiarra ran from his cabin to the deck outside and saw Jack swabbing down the deck. Did he know what he was doing? He wondered. Regardless, he had to stop it immediately. "Boy, come here!"

Jack complied at once, but in his haste, kicked over the water bucket. "Yes, my Captain!"

Santiarra looked disturbed and grabbed Jack's mended arm, "You look ready to return to your regular duties. What say you?"

Careful, Jack! This might be a trap.

"My sight is not what it once was, but if that be your order, my Captain, I am ready for duty."

213

"Good. Then go aloft and give us a clear course. We set sail for home."

"Home, Captain?"

"Virginia! Mr. Bart said that is where you hail from. It was his wish that your mark to this ship be fulfilled three year ago. Now, make haste." The Captain yelled, "Weigh anchors, we sail for the Americas."

Santiarra told the Bosun to bring the ship's supply of rum to his quarters, saying he wanted to secure it. After the last case had been left in his office, he locked the door and opened the first bottle. "Do not think that I don't know what you are planning, my sweet little fishy girl. But this will keep you in place."

He poured the first bottle in and Shera ducked under water to climb onto her sleeping platform in the enclosure. He poured in another bottle, then another, emptying a whole case into the nautilus. His quarters reeked of rum.

Jeremy... Oh Jeremy... Help me, my love. Shera passed out.

"I will, my love," replied Jack Quick.

There was not much in the way of a friendly port for a ship flying the Union Jack, but even less for one flying the Emerald Lady. Two American frigates chased her from the Carolinas to Maryland, where a French man-of-war cut across her path. It hit her with a six-pound smoking cannonball and the men recognized the danger immediately. It was the same as the exploding balls they had used to sink their adversaries.

Thomas Bush-Grabber swept up the searing ball into his arms and it cooked his chest instantly. He dove from the nearest gun port and his heroic splash into the ocean was interrupted by the greater fountain of the explosion, as he rained down on his ship and mates.

The Bosun ordered return fire from the carronade guns. All their guns now fired gunpowder-packed cannonballs, which they had learnt how to make the delay fuses while in the Caymans by soaking old deck lines in pure clear rum, which was much too strong for drinking, then rolling the dry line in mud. Coiled and packed into the cannonball hole as a plug, the cannon's fire would start the fuse burning.

The barrage of exploding cannonballs set the French Man-of-war ablaze and she burnt for hours but continued to fight. The frigates were lighter ships, the Emerald Lady took them out of the battle with a broadside shot to one and the tail gunner sent a ball through the bow of the other. The explosion took half the boat off but not before a marine in the crow's nest put a musket ball in Captain Santiarra's chest. Jack Quick picked off the marine.

The battle waged for two days before the Emerald Lady could finally slip away heavily damaged. Hundreds of men went into the sea, and two of the Queen's maidens with them. And Shera? Oblivious to it all. The heavy rum concentration keeping her intoxicated to the point of hallucinations.

The Bosun and two of the other men lay the Captain in his bed to die in comfort from his wound, Jack being one of them. After the Captain took his last breath, Bart went into the private chamber, quickly followed by Jack, who tried to stop him from looking in the ornate tub. Bart was shocked to see the woman in the golden dress near death in a bath of rum. "What madness be this?"

They wrapped the Captain's body in his bed sheets and tossed him in the corner then the three men removed the girl from the nautilus and lay her on the bed.

Jack said, "Quickly, remove that gold mail from her."

"That be not very gentlemanly," said Bart. "We will wait for her to regain her senses, and provide her with proper clothing."

"I agree with Mr. Quick," said the man with a patch over his right eye. "I say we see what treasure the Captain kept for himself."

"I be Captain now," Bart said and quickly stuck his cutlass in and up the man's torso. "Jack, me boy, best we keep this matter strictly between us two. Until we can find out who and what she be."

"She is a mermaid. And we need to free her now," insisted Jack.

"No doubt," agreed Bart. "But she is in no condition to be thrown back into the sea, boy. Give me a hand in getting these two bodies out of here, and we will head for Island waters. We will lock her in the cabin for the moment. And not a word. Agreed?"

Captain Bart had no intention of returning Shera to the sea for he quickly learnt that the golden dress kept her immobile. And while he allowed Jack to take her a single bucket of seawater to replenish her daily, his plans involved using her powers to turn the Emerald Lady into a proper pirate ship. He was done being a privateer, and with Shera onboard, they could take any ship they came across and plunder to their heart's desire.

He got her cooperation at the tip of his cutlass and a promise to run Jack through to boot. She gave him the location of a British supply ship, which carried five hundred pounds of silver. The reputation of the Emerald Lady was well-known in these seas; her guns having sunk more ships than any other. The British Captain surrendered without a single shot fired. Captain Bart not only took the silver, he took the crew and ship too. They were now wanted by all four nations on the seas.

Captain Bart had a mermaid figurehead carved, similar to the one on the flag. But the mermaid on the figurehead held her sword in both hands and appeared to be charging. Then he had the emerald tub emptied and locked Shera in the figurehead, her new prison. Thus, the Emerald Lady became the flagship of his pirate's armada.

Within two years, Captain Bart had a fleet of ten vessels under his command, with which he raided ships and ports in the Caribbean and Americas alike. Once Captain Bart tasted real power, bestowed on him by the mermaid Shera, he lost all sense of dignity. And his fatherly concerns for Jack swiftly forgotten, he lusted for gold, rum, and blood. The effects a mermaid had on a man, was largely determined by the nature of the man.

Jack served as first mate onboard the Lady, bidding his time and waiting for the right moment to move against Bart and his shipmates. And that moment came when he spotted a dark horizon and got a sense of déjà vu. Like so many years previously, this was a killer storm and he steered the Emerald Lady straight into its heart. Before Captain Bart and the crew knew it, they were being beaten and battered by sea and wind.

In the ensuing confusion, Jack slipped below deck, broke the locks on the doors to the figurehead, and working quickly through the onslaught of the storm, at last cut and chopped through the belt around Shera's waist. Then as he pulled the golden mail over her head and her body was illuminated by a lightning bolt for a second, he was awestruck and immobilized. She was perfect, beautiful, her red hair like a sea of flames curling and engulfing her.

Stay here. You will be safe. She told him.

Shera appeared on deck, amid the men desperately trying to save the ship and themselves, but one by one all stopped their struggles, mesmerized by her exquisiteness. Crazily, they turned on each other, forgetting about the storm, fighting savagely to get to her. Swords and daggers flashed as brightly as the lightning of the storm. Each man blinded by his own desires to ascend the forecastle stairs and claim his prize. Shera stood stolidly, her fiery beauty beaconing them to abandon their duty. Captain Bart used his massive bulk to slash and hack his way through half the crew. A wave rose behind them, and as Shera saw its impending danger, no one else did. It crashed on deck with all its force, taking the Captain, and his bloody sword. Came morning light, the storm had passed, and two handfuls of pirates had survived their brethren, the storm, and Jack Quick.

Shera was quick to return to the deck, dressed in her black and red leather outfit, and announced, "Jack Quick is the new Captain of the Emerald Lady. We, now, are in search of a very special treasure!"

Chapter 14
In Search of Gold

Jack finally established that Shera was the mermaid who
had towed him towards shore after his shipwreck all those
years ago, and at last realized that the treasure she was
seeking was Jeremy Simmons, his father's best friend, and
the man he owed his life to.

Freeing her had also had a profound effect on him;
it cleared his mind and emotions towards her, as he felt a
deep maternal passion from her. He had always been
reminded of his mother in her presence and now that she
was free, it was more than the resemblance he caught
fleeting glimpses of. He could feel that in everything she
had been through, she had never forgotten or abandoned

him, somehow staying connected to him since the sinking of the Rummy Gale.

Their first port of call was Jamaica, the docks clogged with sugar barges waiting for ships to transport their goods to the European continent. The American Revolution or the War for Independence as it was known in the colonies had seriously disrupted the transatlantic routes and trade. As a result, people were angry and information, from the ridiculous to the real, abounded in the streets and along harbors. One needed only mention a name or incident and debates would rage for hours, if not days.

Jack told Shera regrettably, "you search in vain. I saw Jeremy Simmons meet his end beneath the executioner's blade. Had I known that was his head on the chopping block I would have stopped the axe man in his swing."

"You could not have," Shera eased his conscience, "you were but a boy. Any attempt would only have placed your head beside his. But you can help find him now."

"Milady," Jack said, "he has been dead five years. Other than a proper burial, what hope is there?"

She smiled at him now. "Jack, as long as I live so does he. This is our fate."

Jack looked at her with complete confusion, but accepted what she said as true. "Still, it is best the men believe we be in search of real treasure. These men are Godless, soulless spawns of Hell, and not one would willingly cast his lot with a perceived sea-witch's."

221

Shera went into a tavern and asked if anyone would join her crew aboard the Emerald Lady. Every man in the place followed her back to the ship.

Meanwhile, Jack and three of his crew were seeing to another part of business. They paid a visit to the island's governor, who was quick to disclose that he did not know where Mrs. Cutter-Smythe had taken the two chests he sought. However, he also told Jack that she had had a ship, the Abandoned Executioner, a true ship of the line, on the opposite side of the island, and had hastily left with her cargo.

To ensure the governor's silence, Jack had two of the men hold him down while the third cut out his tongue. Then Jack left him with a further warning, "If these men need to come back, it will be your heart they leave with next time."

The pair agreed that the only way to find Jeremy was to locate the ship and have a look at her log. They knew Rehema had only been gone a week during that time, so Jeremy's body and head had to be somewhere in the Caribbean Islands.

As they were leaving Jamaica, Shahira arrived onboard. Without delay, Shera asked her to track down the ship, and both hoped the Queen had not sunk it to keep the secret safe.

Shahira told her, "but we will find it, above or below water. The American Revolution is practically over and the Queen has lost a lot of her supporters, both man and maiden."

"So this is about over for her as well," Jack noticed.

222

Shahira shook her head. "The Queen will sacrifice all our lives to see the curse remain intact. And until every ship is sunk or burning on the shore, she shall continue pushing men to war."

"Then, if we are to go after her flagship, we need to upgrade our weapons, as I imagine she will not be taken without a fight, and a hard one at that. We have been up against Men-of-war before and not fared well at all." Jack continued. "Now this Abandoned Executioner is a hundred-and-four-gun first-rate vessel of the line, but as all ships do, she has one true hazardous shortcoming. Fire. We have to use that to our advantage."

When they arrived at St. Thomas, Jack had the new arsenal ready. Small six-pound balls, hollowed and filled with musket shot and pitch, with six spikes to make the ball stick to the ship if they could not penetrate the thick oak sides. They had been designed for two purposes. First and foremost, to set the ship ablaze. Second, kill anyone around it who might be able to put out the flames. Their plan was to engage the ship in a quick, short skirmish and set her on fire. In the confusion, Shahira would climb aboard and steal the log.

That night, Shahira towed Jack and Shera ashore in a longboat to the British port; if there was any talk of the Executioner, it would be here.

Jack and Shera were complete unknowns, although their dress suggested that they were pirates. Jack wore the leather waistcoat with three holster loops on each side of his chest, a cutlass, and at least one dagger handle showing in his boot. Shera wore leather pants with pistol holsters strapped to each thigh. Her leather coat covering the white silk blouse that was crisscrossed with two more thin leather gun belts. A cutlass hung from her hip and daggers stuck out of her thigh-high boots. If she were not so pretty, men would steer clear of her. But they were drawn to her regardless of the danger she presented.

Shera had had her fill of the world of men, was not about to trust any, swore that she would never be at their mercy again, and kept a hand close to her pistol at all times.

There was not much talk of the Executioner, which had not been seen in these waters in three years, they were told at two places.

At the next tavern, a man approached them without warning, "So it is true, you are looking for her ship."

Shera drew her pistol and the tavern patrons all noticed. Shahira, dressed in a long skirt and blouse that did little to hide that she too was heavily armed, placed a hand on Shera's pistol and lowered the barrel. "Speak smartly now, and be it the truth. What do you know of our business?"

"Milady, do you not know me? I be your First Mate, Sam Brantley."

Shera looked into the man's eyes and there was a vague remembrance of him. "You are older, and hard years they were. But you kept your distance from me in the past. What has emboldened you thus?"

"True, I had my fear of you. But I witnessed the old witch, the one with the sharks' eyes and a disposition to match. I found your company was at least pleasant."

"Ah, that be our mother you speak of," Shahira told him.

"Sorry Ma'am."

"No more than we are," Shera joked and holstered her pistol, "What news have you of the Ol' Crow?"

"The ship and her cargo are far from here. When the Captain met the axe man's blade, Mr. Irons and meself felt compelled to follow, knowing his life is so bound to yours. We snuck aboard with the crew of the Abandoned Executioner and were swept from these waters by a wind most foul. It was so strong, it shivered the timbers and bowed the masts to the point of shattering oak and shredding canvas. We made our first stop in a land of dense jungle and then again on the other side of the world. Each time she went ashore with a chest. The only time I saw her granite turn to flesh."

"We must find that ship, get her logs, and find out where she docked," Jack told the man who seemed to have aged twenty years in the last five.

"You need not find the Executioner to trace her course, I have it in my head. Or rather, on it," Sam Brantley told them as he parted his hair to reveal tattoos on his skull. "But this is only the course that we took. The actual burial place will be written on my mate, Mr. Irons."

"Then take us to him," Jack demanded.

Shera and Shahira both sensed the shift in Brantley's mood and said together, "Mr. Irons is lost, isn't he?"

"The hag took the body into the jungle, more than a day's journey inland before burying Captain Simmons. Henry Irons went with them and had me lay the course on his back, as he sketched this on mine." Sam touched his scalp as he recalled. "Lest either of us forget. Then we continued on the Devil's wind to some unknown island where the Sun touched down for the night. Henry went ashore again with the head in a box. Neither she nor the party returned. I fear she left them in the same hole as Captain Simmons."

"It be a fact, dead men tell no tales," commented Jack.

"Aye. Suspicions and too many questions about my head markings caused me to jump ship in the land of the Moors; I did not want that witch coming for me. I worked my way back here."

"Well, good fortune for us." Jack observed. "So, we can use the map on your head to take us to the shores and the map inside your head to take us to Jeremy's body. Then we will go for his head."

"Even if I could remember the drawing, it was incomplete. I have a hazy memory of a path, but without land markings it will be meaningless."

"Lead us to the landing and we will have a thousand maidens search that land inch by inch until his body is found." Shahira told him. "The island will be much easier, it's an island. Sam Brantley, do we make a sketch of your head or do you lead us there?"

"I would be honored to sail with you, Miladies."

After shaving Sam Brantley's head, they sailed south.

Although Shahira had told them that they would call upon a thousand maidens to take up the search, the truth was that there were not many left. The past eight years of Rehema's warmongering had decimated their population, leaving a couple of hundreds scattered throughout the world. And since a maiden only spawned every hundred years after reaching maturity, a single maiden rarely had more than seven maidens in her lifetime. It would take millennia to replenish their numbers. She felt, as did so many of them lately, that the age of Maidens was coming to a close. The very thing the Queen had accused men of doing, had come to pass by her hand. Still, they had to try.

Sam Brantley hoped that Henry Irons had managed to escape the Queen's clutches and somehow survived on the island. But it would be months before he could expect an answer and he had the nagging feeling that the Executioner would not allow them to make land at either site. He was haunted by the cruelty onboard, as she was not operated like any other ship in His Majesty's Royal Navy. Her crews were prisoners and officers mad with talk of gold, worse than any pirate ship on the high seas.

"They attacked ships without warning in the night, robbing and sinking them, without mercy for the crews. It was like the business of the two chests was a poison that

infected the Captain, his officers, and the crew." Sam
Brantley cautioned the trio.

For months, they followed the globe tattooed on
Sam's head until reaching a large bay towards the skinny
end of South America. There, Shahira and a dozen men set
out in two longboats for the interior. Without a map, it
was like looking for a drop of water in the ocean, a vain
attempt. But if they could find one part of the body then
the other would be easier to locate. Perhaps the island,
being a limited area might be the place to start, and
between herself and Shera they could get lucky and then
return here for the body. But it would take six months, at
least, to reach the island from the present location.

The Emerald Lady sailed around the stormy seas of Cape
Horn then northwest through the south Pacific, hopping
from island chain to island chain. On some of the Islands,
Shera was recognized and treated as a returning goddess,
but on others, she advised the men to stay clear of. "Flesh
eating people," she warned.

As they neared their destination, Shera was certain
her mother had buried the head chest on one of the
cannibalistic island and told Sam that that had probably
been the reason why the shore party never returned. From
the land's position on his skin, she concluded that they
should sight the island near New Caledonia. That part of
the world had only recently been explored by westerners.

Sam slept on deck instead of the crew berths below, as he had previously awakened to islanders aboard their ships and developed a healthy fear for being surprised and overpowered. But what had been far worse, was to awaken to find no one left on deck. The night watch and helmsman spirited away in the night by the Flesh Eaters.

But his far graver concern was what he had been part of, the Abandoned Executioner attacking unsuspecting ships in the night. He had no wish to run into her as the target of her weapons. Her massive size, wide arrangement of guns and armaments made her an insurmountable foe. Her gunnery crew was well-practiced in disabling a ship within minutes, taking down its sails and destroying the rudder. Dead in the water, a ship would be bled by grapple fire and marines in the nest. Surrender was the only option, and it too led to death.

Jack doubled the night watch and had two marine gunners in the riggings. Shera returned to her nautilus, feeling renewed energy and surrounded by those who loved and protected her. Her powers were strong and she had accepted the fact that her mother was a monster. Now, she needed to do whatever it took to end her reign of tyranny. And as she contemplated these issues, she suddenly felt the Abandoned Executioner turn towards them.

Sam Brantley picked up the slapping of waves on a bow almost as soon as Shera did. He had heard it turn into battle position so often that he immediately spotted the craft heading their way. He piped one low long whistle that called men to battle stations; all responded, immediately and silently. They planned to look unaware of the upcoming battle and beat the Abandoned Executioner to the punch.

Jack, he is maneuvering to becalm you. Stay to the port tact and head to the shallows of the reef.

Jack heard and obeyed, able to keep a good distance between them and the Executioner. The Lady caught the cross wind first and raced forward then swung right and cut across the Executioner's bow. He ordered the guns to life and the Emerald Lady disappeared behind a cloud of burning powder.

The bow of the Executioner was struck repeatedly by the six-pounders and those that hit lighter-built deck structures went through to explode and spread burning pitch everywhere. Those that hit the heavy built hull, stuck and exploded, causing small holes and setting the exterior on fire. The Executioner responded with her long guns. The cannonballs flew over the deck missing the two masts but punched holes in two of the Lady's sails.

Jack ordered the starboard Devastator to fire its load of three rows of four six-pounders. Mostly, the cannonballs hit the hull, stuck, exploded and sent a river of burning musket balls flowing up the side and showering the deck with fiery lead pellets. One cannonball found its way into the gun port and nailed the gunner to the deck before exploding.

The Emerald Lady swung head on to the Executioner, presenting a narrow target to her guns, the forward Devastator firing a regular exploding ball which penetrated the broadside of the Executioner at the second gun deck. The explosion was disastrous to the port gunnery crews. Those who were able to return fire were totally ineffectual.

Continuing her turn until she was port to port, the Lady fired all her guns, the Devastator with its twenty-pound load and all six-pound shots taking advantage of the weakened hull. Another massive explosion rocked the Abandoned Executioner, turning it into a floating inferno. Her crew having to abandon the fight and pump water from her bilge tanks to save their ship returned no fire.

Jack ordered a careful retreat from the water while they only suffered minor damage then resumed course, and replaced the two sails quickly. The Abandoned Executioner might be able to get the fires under control, but even if she did, she would be in no condition to follow them. That was what Jack thought. He was very wrong.

At morning light, the lookouts saw the Abandoned Executioner under full sail and closing in on them. She was still fuming smoke from her decks, but she was ready for battle. Cannonballs from her bow guns whistled past the Emerald Lady.

Jack ordered the aft guns loaded and the aft Devastator to have its hull-crushing cannonballs ready.

A second round of cannon fire splashed down around the Lady, one ball slamming into the weather deck, and the repercussion threw five men overboard.

Shera reached out to one of the crew below her tending the aft Devastator. *Pull the rear hatch line on the wall ahead of you.*

He immediately grabbed the rope, not knowing where it went or what it did and pulled as hard as he could. The water-tight hatch Jeremy had cut into the Sea Queen when she had sat on the bottom, opened and a rush of water flooded the hull. The Emerald Lady slowed and sank five-feet deeper in the water. Seventy-two-pound cannonballs from the Executioner's starboard guns meant to crush her, flew overhead and landed in the water.

Fire! Fire! Fire now.

The entire crew of the Emerald Lady heard the orders. The rear Devastator thundered its cannonball into the Executioner just above the waterline, the explosions causing the sea to erupt around her. Her lower decks caved in along the entire waterline on her starboard and she keeled over on her port side, which had a massive gash from the previous night's battle. The Executioner rolled completely over belly up and began to sink; the sea around her boiling with white foam. It went down in minutes.

The entire crew of the Emerald Lady cheered then fell silent as they realized that not a single man aboard the other vessel had survived the sinking. No one had ever seen a ship go down like that before, and they knew they never would again. Shera became grief-stricken, having given the order that cost so many lives.

The Emerald Lady arrived at an island known simply as The Rock. Jack, Shera, and Sam went ashore with six men, and were soon met by two dozen spear-toting men in war paint and little else.

"Flesh Eaters." Shera announced.

"Can you communicate with them?" Jack asked.

"Their minds are blocked and have only one thought in them," she told them.

"I think I can speak their language," Sam said, getting ready to draw his pistol.

"Right idea, but not loud enough. Besides, the others would kill us. I, however, left orders." Jack waved his right hand above his head. The ship's port cannons thundered a cloud of white smoke.

Visibly afraid, the group of warriors kneeled and laid their spears on the sand.

"This way," said Shera and as she passed the first man and tapped him on the head. He got up at once and followed them. "This one is the leader. It is his hut we are going to."

The six men carrying shovels and axes followed the rest of the tribe.

Arriving at the chief's hut, Sam stared at one wall, "Is that what I think it is?"

"I'm sorry, but it is," Jack said and grabbed Henry Irons' tattooed back skin from the wall.

Sam drew his pistol and pointed it at the chief's head, "Filthy savage, you will pay for this."

"Two days ago you cheered the death of over three hundred men. Is he really more of a savage then you are?" Shera scolded him.

Shera ran her hands over the dry skin, reading its history. She told them that the group had survived two months before being overtaken, visibly enough time for the men to have completed the tattoo, as there were two trails on Henry Irons' back and Sam had pointed to the left one and announced that he had started that one. They abandoned the pursuit thereof and settled on the one to the right, which turned out to be not too far inland. They started digging in earnest at the end of the trail, and unearthed the small chest.

Hundreds of miles away, Shahira and Raakel swam with a small group of maidens through the South Pacific carrying the chest containing Jeremy's body. As soon as they arrived, all climbed aboard and disappeared into the Captain's cabin. When the full moon rose high in the sky, they removed his body and head from the chests and placed them in the nautilus with Shera.

Tears of joy and ire streamed down her face and fused with seawater. Their goal finally accomplished, the small group departed from the chamber as silently as they had arrived, leaving the two lovers alone, and returned to the sea.

Maidens from around the world converged on the ship, swimming around it in concentric patterns, each circle in a different direction, and at different angles. They leapt into the air, over decks and sails, diving and falling back into the water without making a single ripple. And once again, the ship was lined with crystals, nearly every inch of deck covered with colorful stones of all shapes and sizes.

The crew was awestruck and terrified simultaneously by the activities, none venturing a word to query the goings-on, especially when at the highest moon the Emerald Lady was bathed in green light and at the same time radiated a green beam of its own through the hull. The crew prayed to whatever or whomever they imagined was a higher power and might be listening to them, and there was no sleep aboard the ship that night.

At morning light, Jack Quick was ecstatic to relinquish command to an alive and healthy Captain Jeremy Simmons. Although the crew had never seen what had been in the chest retrieved from the island or the other brought onboard by the mermaids, they had no doubt that it had been the Captain, separated at the neck. And even if none would admit it to one another when toeing the line that morning, all thought that life at sea was becoming more unpredictable than they had ever imagined it could be and all wished they had taken up a life of farming.

The First Mate, Jack 'Quick' Roggies asked, "Captain Simmons, what orders have you for your crew?"

"I had a very long time to plan." Jeremy gave him a crooked smile. "So first, every man looks like he can use a drink. Bosun Brantley, open the ship's rum supply and let each man drink his fill three times over."

"Yes sir. Starting with meself, I assure you."

"Then once we are standing again, and have a clear head," Jeremy drew his sword and stabbed it into the deck, "I am going to snare that witch of a Queen, Rehema. And watch her squirm."

Chapter 15
Through Watery Eyes

"Do you not thirst for rum, my love?" Shera asked.

"I hunger and thirst for only you."

"I was so lost without you. And now, as much as it pains me to say it, my mother must be caught and made to pay. She has taken so many lives, my sisters, your brothers, she cannot be allowed..."

Jeremy interjected. "I know your pain, my darling, because while you could only see darkness through my eyes, I could see every moment of every day through yours. And during all your suffering you have not been corrupted. Your purity has helped to cleanse my mind."

"So... what? You want to hide somewhere, or forgive her for all the harm she has done?" Shera was angry, but not with Jeremy, at herself for not having listened to him before. As presently, he seemed to be planning to do what she had originally wanted to do; and that had led to so much unnecessary death.

"No, not forgive her. And definitely not allow her to continue," Jeremy held Shera close, feeling her heart beating rapidly, all the years of painful loneliness pouring out of her. He took it all in, savoring the moment. How long had he lain in the grave wishing for nothing more than to touch her, yearning for the moisture of her tears when she hurt, longing for the warmth of her breath as the cold of the grave closed in on him. "We will do to her what she did to us. We will take away what she loves and desires most," he announced.

"She loves no one. And desires nothing but destruction," Shera lamented. "Pain is all she knows."

"You are right about that," Jeremy agreed, "But she does love, she loves power, craves it, and cannot live without it. So, she will taste the pain of loss. We will trap her and turn her human and she will surrender all her powers."

"You tried that before," Shera reminded him, "And she severed your head for it. Do you really want that experience again?"

"Ha ha ha... huh, yes, my plan was ill conceived then, but I had a long time to revise certain aspects. My biggest mistake was that I tried to trap her out of water, where she manipulated the weak minds of men. I know better now."

"I hope so," Shera said, "Because I cannot go through another ten years like that again."

"Don't you fear, my darling. Never again."

While his men spent three days drunk out of their minds, Jeremy and Shera spent the time in the nautilus, feeding off each other's energy. The more they tried to satisfy their desires the more they wanted and the greater their desire for one another became. He recalled the first calming kiss. She remembered the love pouring forth from his heart the first time she had touched him. They found it endlessly more satisfying, both more alive, and more connected than ever. They shared a single mind, heart, and soul. Knowing the other one's darkness and loneliness had created an understanding the Queen with all her powers could neither do nor undo. They sunk to the bottom of the tub wrapped in delight, and remained there trading air from their mouths until they fell asleep.

And for those three days, maidens circled the ship incessantly, blocking any knowledge of Jeremy's return from the Queen. All mermaids who had survived the American Revolution were now firmly set against Rehema. Fighting alongside men had shown them that they were not their enemies, as most wanted nothing more than a peaceful life and an easy death. And although they still believed in a single ruler, they also knew that blind faith and the wrong one could lead to disaster for all. But hopefully, now, it would be Jeremy and Shera who would lead both man and maiden to peace. All were ready to collaborate to end the Queen's rule, and choose another to head them.

Jeremy addressed the maidens from the Emerald Lady's deck. "I need you to track down your Queen. But do not engage her, no need for anyone else to die."

"We can call her to Usea Maya," someone suggested. "If we do it all together, she will not be able to resist. Then we can demand she lift her curses and surrender her power."

"I beg of you, do not move against your Queen. She may not have power over you but she still carries sway over men, and she is likely to go to Usea Maya with warships," Jeremy warned. "Just keep me informed of her whereabouts, and I will do the rest."

All agreed.

The sinking of the Abandoned Executioner meant that Rehema needed to build more warships, yet, she was also very much aware that the age of the sail ship was coming to an end. They were vulnerable to fire and far too explosive. Feeling the winds of change, she had returned to the newly formed United States of America. Working with men to preserve the natural order of life, as she called it, she kept pointing out that the fledging nation would need leaders to keep things the way they were. In

Richmond, at the Commonwealth of Virginia, she kept arguing that the war had left the northern colonies beyond powerful, poised to take over control of all commerce, and hence would dictate the fate of the southern colonies.

Then, she rushed off to New York, where she told a delegation that the United States needed to solidify its power in the New World. They needed a mightier battleship to protect its coast and project its authority from north to south. They needed to expel the European influence from this side of the world.

England was not left out of her schemes. There, she spurred the idea that any and every American merchant ship and crew was and could be pressed into service as British citizens. She led the argument that the American Revolutionary War did not end England's colonial rights at sea.

She further fueled the flames of war around Europe by suggesting to the new leader of France to take total control of his government. Telling Napoleon that the British were at their weakest, that if he defeated them, the world would be his. She was determined to see the world of men burn, their capitals either falling to her rule or be reduced to rubble. Her power over the maidens had faded with the deaths she had coldheartedly caused at sea, but it had strengthened tenfold on land. In her various forms as Admiral, General, Lord, and Lady she continued to twist and turn men's minds cruelly to her will.

In the Americas, she implemented a new technology into her ship designs, steam power to replace the fickle wind, and iron-plating to counter Jeremy's exploding cannonballs. Her ships would be smaller, lighter, and more agile. Armed with exploding shells, these would be more than a match for the Emerald Lady. And this time, she decided, there would be certain death for both Jeremy and Shera, and anyone else who dared to stand against her, on ground or in water.

She would sooner turn both land and sea to blood before she gave up her power to those two and that disgusting thing they called love. She sensed them moving against her yet again and it infuriated her, driving her to the point of madness, and beyond.

But Rehema was not to imagine that she alone was privy to the winds of change. Change was contagious and those who understood the benefits of progress were quick to grasp it with both hands, and so it was with Jeremy. Somehow perceiving Rehema's need to beat him at every cost, he had sent Raakel and Shahira ahead to Germany, where they had gone to the city of Hamburg on the Elbe River to bring plans of a new type of ship he called the Golden Whale.

Under the protection of several mermaids in his crew, who scouted the seas against ambushes wherever they went, he sailed around the world for two years while waiting for his whale to be completed. And along the way, in partnership, they collected the unique ammunition specifically needed to defeat Rehema. Maidens located the sunken golden treasures, men hauled them to the surface and Jeremy had most of the gold melted for his secret weapon. And while they busied themselves thus, the German ship-builder had more than enough time to assemble the coal-burning submersible ship.

The Whale looked like no other vessel of the day. In fact, it looked like two ships, one turned upside down on top of the other. Or perhaps even like a flattish fat shark more than a whale, but she needed to surface to breathe, so she was aptly named. Her exterior was smooth, thanks to her golden skin plated to the wooden frame, which had been built from bamboo to reduce weight. And although the plating had been intended to withstand a strike from Rehema, it was still too thin and the wood too light to give much protection against cannon fire.

But, Jeremy observed, the Golden Whale was close to invisible, and with the sea protecting her, enemy ships were barely aware that she was nearby. They sailed so low in the water as to be almost undetectable, and when fully submerged, they were completely unseen from the surface, black paint on her topside made sure of that. Furthermore, she carried a new type of cannon, six of them. Instead of using a charge and ball, these used compressed steam from the boiler for a barrage of golden balls out of their gun-barrels. She had four forward-facing guns on the lower deck, two on the upper deck loaded with golden nets, and the secret weapon mounted in the front section. Her body contained the boilers and mechanisms for controlling fin size and speed, and in the last section was her tail, which swished back and forth to propel the vessel like a shark on the hunt.

The Germans saw the design as impractical and prone to failure. It used steam to work the tail as well as control the water in the ballast tanks which allowed the ship to float and dive, but if the boiler failed, the ship would sink like a rock, and with a hull as fragile as an eggshell, it was a combination built for a disaster. Only a madman would go to sea in such a vessel. But Jeremy knew something he could not tell the German ship-builders. This ship had been built for the sole purpose of catching a single mermaid.

Jeremy needed only six men to operate the vessel, so he asked the crew for volunteers. Sam Brantley stepped forward first, with a hearty, "Yo Ho, Sir!" Jack Quick also stepped forward, but Jeremy rejected his application, telling him that the Emerald Lady was his henceforth. And, Jeremy noted further; he needed Jack above water to drive the Queen from her ship and back into the sea, where she would believe herself invincible.

Raakel, Shahira, and Aberash, who had suddenly appeared on the dock, completed the crew. Jeremy protested but Aberash was quick to point out that he needed them, as only mermaids could save the rest of the crew if his plan failed to capture Rehema and she sank this beautiful golden tin-can of a vessel.

Jeremy could not argue with the logic, but was also quick to tell her that he did not intend to lose anyone and had planned an emergency exit in the event of Rehema indeed sinking them. After his first shipwreck, he had thought long and hard of a way to survive at sea, so in view of those challenges, they now carried bottled air and a hose they could breathe from and through. Nonetheless, Shera, Jack, and Sam were thankful the maidens had joined the crew.

Jeremy took additional precautionary measures against attacks from Rehema's ships. He knew that forcing her to fight, would compel them in turn to sink her ships first, so he carried wooden cannonballs loaded with explosives that would rise to the surface when fired from the Golden Whale and exploded the moment they came into contact with a hull. As he had noted from the sinking of the Abandoned Executioner by Jack, an explosion at or below the waterline meant a sure end to a ship.

Additionally, the Emerald Lady carried golden grapple shot and nets for her small guns. Between the two ships, they were determined to return the world to its rightful course. And it was not long before they were put to the test.

Three British Royal Navy frigates advanced on the Emerald Lady as she sailed out of the North Sea. The maidens on both vessels declared that Rehema was not onboard. Instead, she was somewhere close by with full control of the crews and intent on sinking the Emerald Lady.

As the three steam-powered frigates charged ahead, the Golden Whale dove under the Emerald Lady and from her submerged position fired six wooden balls. The compressed steam ejected water, charged her barrels and the balls rolled forward from the boiling sea directly into the warships' path. The unconventional attack left the three Captains confused as to what it meant and what would happen next. They soon found out.

As hulls struck the black spiky balls bobbing in the waves, watery swords pierced the bottom of the ships. Bows lifted out of the water, throwing sailors tumbling backwards then slammed back into the water and broke away from the rest of the vessels. With nowhere to go, men scrambled over the sides of the doomed ships. Not too far, the Queen was well aware of this first encounter with the Golden Whale and her resounding defeat.

The Emerald Lady fished as many sailors from the icy waters as was possible and the maidens retrieved the longboats that were still floatable to send the men on their way home. Jack and Jeremy had agreed that from now on they would take as few lives as possible during these encounters, but knew also that Rehema would make no such provisions. In contrast, she would send as many ships and men to their deaths as she could while trying to destroy their two craft.

Maidens were tracking the Queen south, heading for the French fleet. Eight first rate ships of the line and six frigates were being called to action by Rehema. The Emerald Lady and the Golden Whale turned west to sail across the Atlantic. They would not take her on with an armada, cause untold damage, and pointless deaths. Instead, they had to coerce her to come to them, alone, to face them on a one to one basis. The American Navy was tiny in comparison to any of the European countries, so fighting in the New World waters gave them the best odds when facing Rehema.

Meanwhile, under Aberash's orders, a group of maidens beat Rehema to the French fleet and took control of the ships, denying her their firepower. Thwarted, she turned towards the American fleet in the west. She could have easily beaten the two vessels across the ocean singlehandedly, but not with her sisters colluding en masse. Disturbingly, it seemed as if they had already gained control of all the craft she had her eye on. But that hardly discourage her, she would just have to take on the Emerald Lady and the Golden Whale alone because she was not without resources.

With all her vessels lost to her, she turned to the Cutter Shipyard to finish building one more ironclad ship, so she would be ready for them when they crossed the Atlantic. Confident and arrogant, she proceeded to taunt her sisters and daughters. *You want me, here I am. Come and get me. I promise you all a painful death.*

The British fleet took position to the north, along the Canadian provinces, and the French fleet along the southern coast near Savannah. The Emerald Lady approached Boston harbor alone and the ironclad Steel Eel, steamed out to engage her. She had a rotatable main turret in the middle of the ship as her main weaponry and was further armed with two forward twelve-pounder cannons and two rear-facing ten-pounders. She was also too low in the water for the Emerald Lady's Devastator guns to be effective, so she would have to rely on her deck guns. The Lady aimed them up and began lobbing shells at the ironclad.

Unsurprisingly, they had no effect on the Steel Eel, the cannonballs bouncing harmlessly into the ocean. Her turret gun fired and struck the Emerald Lady broadside, the cannonball breaking through and ricocheting off the far side. Registering success, the turret turned and fired a second shot. Jack ordered the flood gate open and the Emerald Lady was quickly pulled down. The cannonball sailed through the riggings, exploded in her sails, and took off the top main mast. Flaming wooden stakes rained down on the crew, her sails falling in a veil of fire. The turret turned again and the gun lowered. Rehema was about to give the order for the final shot.

An exploding cannonball in her midsection will tear the ship apart. Rehema announced.

So will six of our cannonballs beneath your hull, sister. Aberash responded.

Ah, sister, you have come to die with these worthless men.

Jeremy fired all six guns at a quarter pressure. The cannonballs left the barrels and rose straight to the surface and as Aberash had warned, they struck the Steel Eel underneath, where she was unprotected by the steel. The ship was instantly torn apart and seeing no other recourse, Rehema transformed and slipped between the fractures in the hull, trying to swim away, injured and trailing blood.

Jeremy ordered the four lower guns loaded with the golden grapple and firing at full pressure, they caught Rehema in a cloud of golden pellets. Each one that struck causing mind-numbing pain to surge through her body, piercing and tumbling her. The Emerald Lady fired the two top guns, her golden nets flying through the air, towards the helpless Queen.

She twisted and turned, trying to avoid the capturing nets but became entangled in one then another. A third weighed her down and she sank to the bottom of the Boston Harbor, unable to move. Jeremy surfaced the Golden Whale and quickly dove into the water with his bottled air and hose strapped to his back. Swimming to the Queen, he saw maidens closing in all around her. Wrapping a line around the netting, he returned to the surface and threw Jack the other end of the line, who hauled her from the water like the morning catch, bleeding, defeated, and humiliated. When aboard the

Emerald Lady, she was chained into the same golden mail she had forced Shera to wear for years.

While none of the maidens called for her death they cheered her imprisonment. A cave on a hillside, far from the sea, on a deserted island had been chosen, and none felt any particular pity towards her incarceration.

The Emerald Lady, docked in the peaceful bay, and her crew witnessed the celebrations as mermaids jumped and frolicked in the water, relieved to be rid of their wayward Queen.

More maidens gathered as the full moon rose higher, singing and splashing tails against the water all night, celebrating the end of the Evil Rehema's reign, as she had now been dubbed.

At sunrise, Jeremy was holding Shera in his arms.

"I don't feel any different." Shera said then shoved him over the side with her arms still wrapped around him. They hit the water with a loud splash and as they sank, Shera swished her tail and raced through the water with him. Inhaling water through her nose, she blew sweet intoxicating air into his lungs.

As she did flips, twists, and spins, he wrapped his arms around her tightly. Then she dove deep into the darkness of the ocean, through an opening in a mountain, down dark corridors, and up into a pool.

Jeremy recognized the cavern at once. Usea Maya, the home of the mermaids. The place Shera had been banned from when the curse was imposed. It was even more beautiful through his own eyes. He was the first and most likely the only human to see the spectacular rainbows projected from the crystalline walls. Clouds of colors circled and rose above him. The chambers echoed with the beating of tails, but there were far fewer in this hall. The last place he had been before the mermaids was dull and dim, but there had been maidens on every ledge, and as high up as one could see. Here they occupied only the lower tiers, a dozen or so levels. But still he could hear their voices inside his head. They were all calmer, happier, and proclaiming Shera as their new Queen.

I thank you all for your faith in me but I cannot be your Queen. I am going to go inland for good to live with the man I love.

Wait a moment, Shera. Who said I want you to live with me on land?

The cavern was awash in shocked response to both declarations.

Jeremy explained himself. *This is the life you were meant to have. And it is the life I fought hard to return you to. You cannot give it up now. Besides, I rather like this little island. So, I think I will stay right here. With you.*

There was riotous noise ringing out of the old volcano in the Caribbean.

The navies of the world settled their difference at the negotiating tables and everyone hoped peace would prevail, at least for a time.

Jack, who had transported Rehema to her prison and then removed the golden mail, bid them a warm goodbye and they wished him a safe return before he sailed away on the Emerald Lady searching for new adventures.

The maidens assigned to look after Rehema's needs, were warned to always be polite and treat her as she had never treated anyone else. They complied, took her food and water, but always made certain she was safely locked away and remained atop the mountain in the cave.

Jeremy built a comfortable cabin in the sparse forest next to a pool on Usea Maya, where he and Shera lived in some seclusion on the island, and where, six months after Shera's crowning as Queen, she gave birth to a maiden. The first between man and maiden, and a great astonishment to all, as maidens who mated with men always gave birth to human offspring. Some had the mental and healing abilities of their mothers, but never any of their physical traits. Seemingly, Shera had already been pregnant at the lifting of the curse, so no one was certain if that had any bearing in the awe they all felt towards this new wonder. But whatever the explanation, Zabella had it all, transforming to maiden in the water and into a perfect and adorable little girl out of it. Happily,

James L Hill

Shera returned to the sea every full moon, with Jeremy in her arms.

The End

About The Author

A native New Yorker, born and raised in the Bronx, James L Hill spent his adolescence years in Fort Apache, the South Bronx 41st precinct during the 60's, during a time when you needed to have a gang to go to the store. Raised on blues, soul, and rock and roll gave him the heart of a flower child. Educated by the turmoil of Vietnam, Civil Rights, and the Sexual Revolution produced a gladiator. Realizing the precariousness of life gave him an adventurous outlook and willingness to try anything once, and if it did not kill him, maybe twice.

12 years of Catholic education and a couple of years in college spread between wild drug induce euphoric years, which did not kill him, gave James an unique moral compass that swings in any direction it wants. A scientific mind and a spirit that nothing is impossible if you want it bad enough guides his writings. He enjoys traveling to new places and seeing what life has to offer.

James began writing short stories and poetry back in his early years. In his twenties moved on to novels. He worked in the financial industry and later got a degree in computer programming, his other love. James has a successful career as a software engineer designing, developing and maintaining systems for the government and the private sector. He has been programming for nearly forty years in various languages.

After years in the computer world he returned to his first love, unleashing the characters in his head. Still a hopeless insomniac, he feels free to pound out plots. James L Hill is a prolific storyteller writing crime stories, fantasies, and science fiction, with a slant on the dark side of life.

Killer With A Heart is the first adult crime novel in the Killer series for Bulletproof Morris 'Mojo' Johnson.

The Emerald Lady is the first novel in the fantasy Gemstone Series.

Pegasus: A Journey To New Eden, his science fictions deal with the emotional effects of technology, and answers the question, "How do I feel about nuclear war?"

Married with six kids, eleven grandchildren lives in Virginia Beach.

RockHill Publishing LLC

There are some lessons that only time can teach,
but you do not learn talent,
you only perfect it over time.

www.rockhillpublishing.com

CHECK OUT OUR OTHER TITLES:

ADULT FICTION:

Killer With A Heart

Killer With Three Heads

FANTASY:

The Emerald Lady

ROMANCE:

Knight Kisses

Love & Madness

SCIENCE FICTION:

Pegasus: A Journey To New Eden

Gemstone Series
Book Two
The Ruby Cradle

It is the turn of the nineteenth century. The industrial age
has begun. Steam-powered ships have taken over the
oceans. Factories are going up across Europe and America.
There is a resurgence of activity in the castles in the
mountains and when the Crimean War breaks out Zabella
is sent to her grandmother, Rehema, to learn about the
dragons.

Rehema mentally transcends the girl to the First Split
(1000 A.D.), the wars her mother, Apollonia, fought to
destroy the dragons as they had spread across Asia, Africa,
and Europe. It began as they built castles and started
controlling men with gold. The dragons have led the
Romans, Egyptians, and Chinese empires over the
centuries. The dragons turn Molytans into Ogres as their
generals who lead huge armies and protect them when
their powers wane at night.

New dragons are created in Europe and now threaten the
balance of power in the world. The world of the dragon is
one of destruction. They take over an area and cause wars
until all is in ruins. Dragons cannot be killed but can be

drained of power causing them to turn into ruby-like stones. Only a dragon can consume another dragon, increasing its power. Or so it seems.

Apollonia becomes a sorceress and can retain her power for years out of water with the help of her sisters. She raises a champion in France to battle the growing threat from England's Cockerot and Russia's Deyhezas. After destroying a Castle in the Alps and capturing its dragon in the Ruby Cradle, Nathan, the Dragon Killer, confronts the English at the Battle of Hastings. Apollonia returns to the sea and spawns Rehema and her two sisters. Afterwards she returns to the world of men to continue the hundred-year war and is burned at the stake as Joan of Arc.

Zabella knows she must prepare men to fight and destroy the dragons before the world is at war once more. She knows dragons can be killed.

Look forward to The Ruby Cradle – Book Two of the Gemstone Series

CPSIA information can be obtained
at www.ICGtesting.com
Printed in the USA
LVHW080517250520
656529LV00009B/195